Chelsea and the Alien Invasion

Best Friends

#14

Chelsea and the Alien Invasion

Hilda Stahl

CROSSWAY BOOKS • WHEATON, ILLINOIS
A DIVISION OF GOOD NEWS PUBLISHERS

Chelsea and the Alien Invasion

Copyright © 1993 by Word Spinners, Inc.

Published by Crossway Books
        a division of
        Good News Publishers
        1300 Crescent Street
        Wheaton, Illinois 60187.

Cover illustration: Paul Casale

Art Direction/Design: Mark Schramm

First printing, 1993

Printed in the United States of America

ISBN 0-89107-749-9

01		00		99		98		97		96		95		94		93
15	14	13	12	11	10	9	8	7	6	5	4	3	2	1

To Marissa Pajot

Contents

1

Mike

Scowling, Chelsea McCrea stood at the head of the basement stairs and shouted, "Mike, come up here now!" She was baby-sitting her eight-year-old brother when she really wanted to be across the street with Hannah Shigwam talking about special valentines for extra-special people—mainly boys.

"Do you hear me, Mike?" He was probably playing his video game on the big-screen TV in their basement rec room. Playing video games was his second favorite thing to do; practicing gymnastic routines was his first. Chelsea frowned. Why didn't he answer her? "You did not finish cleaning your room like you're supposed to!" One of the rules in their house was that her two brothers and herself had to keep their rooms clean and tidy. Mike's gym clothes were in a ball on his carpet, his dresser drawers were hanging open, and his wastebasket was tipped over, which explained why everything was scattered across his floor.

Chelsea stamped her foot. "Don't make me come get you, Mike!"

Still he didn't answer. That wasn't like Mike at all. A shiver trickled down Chelsea's spine. "Mike? Are you down there?" she called softly. No answer.

She ran down the stairs and looked around the empty rec room. He wasn't sitting in front of the big-screen TV or raiding the small refrigerator. The pool table and the Ping-Pong table looked as if they hadn't been used in a long time. She frowned thoughtfully. "Where are you, Mike?"

She dashed back upstairs and called throughout the house. It wasn't like Mike to just disappear. He wouldn't run to the corner store outside their subdivision, The Ravines, where their brother Rob was working after school. Mike was always very obedient. So, where was he?

She ran to his bedroom to see if he'd left a clue to where he'd gone. No clues. She sighed heavily and looked out the window. The ground was party covered with snow. She looked past the yard next door and on toward a grove of trees at the edge of the subdivision. Lately he'd been spending time among those trees. He said he liked to play there and that he'd found a new friend. Maybe he'd gone there without telling her. She knotted her fists. "He better not have!"

Downstairs she checked the closet for his winter boots and jacket. They were gone. Sighing heavily, she pulled on her boots and bright green coat. She flipped her long red hair over her shoulders and let it cascade down her back.

She walked out the back door and cut across the yard of their new neighbors. She hadn't met any of them yet and didn't know their names. If only she could call the Best Friends to go with her to look for Mike! The Best Friends were Hannah Shigwam who lived across the street, Roxie Shoulders who lived right next door, and Kathy Aber who lived a block outside The Ravines. They met almost every day to talk, help each other, share a verse from the Bible, and pray for each other and for anyone else they knew needed prayer. They did good deeds for others, and they had fun shopping together and playing together. She couldn't survive without the Best Friends, and she knew they all felt the same way.

The cold February wind blew against Chelsea, and she wished she had put on her knit cap. She hadn't needed one in Oklahoma, but here in Michigan the winter was too cold to go without one. Just last month she'd helped Hannah and her neighbors, the Griggs family, build an igloo just like Eskimos had once lived in. The igloo was still standing, but it didn't look as good as before. The sun was warm enough a few days last week to melt it a little. But Roxie's dad said the igloo would probably stand until the end of March.

Why hadn't Mike gone to the igloo instead of the trees? Chelsea stopped short. Maybe he had! Mike liked sitting inside the snow house.

Frowning, Chelsea looked back over her shoulder. She was almost to the grove of winter-bare trees, so she'd look there first. If he wasn't there, she'd look in the igloo. She rammed her gloved hands into her jacket pockets. "You're in real trouble now, Mike McCrea!"

Wind flipped her hair and turned her nose and cheeks red as she ran past the area where a new house was being built near the trees.

She stopped just inside the grove and looked around. She saw fallen branches and a few pines among the leafless trees. A squirrel leaped from branch to branch, then stopped and chattered noisily. A few birds flew from the branches and out across the snowy field Roxie had told her had once been a pasture.

Suddenly a scream rang through the air. Chelsea's heart stopped, then hammered so hard she thought it would leap through her jacket. Who had screamed? And why? She had to see if someone was in trouble, even though she felt like running home as fast as she could.

Silently praying for God's help, Chelsea walked toward the scream. Her steps sounded loud in her own ears. Dare she call out for Mike? She shook her head. She might be walking into danger. She couldn't let anyone know she was there.

Up ahead she caught a movement of red. Her pulse leaped. Mike had a red jacket. She hesitated, then kept walking, careful not to snap any fallen twigs.

She caught the flash of red again, and then Mike ran into sight. She gasped. His face was white with fear, and he was crying. What had happened to him?

She ran toward him, and he ran toward her. He acted as if he didn't see her. Just before they collided she yelled, "Mike!"

He stopped short, then flung himself at her and clung so tightly to her she could barely breathe. She felt him tremble as he sobbed against her. She shivered in sudden fear. "What's wrong, Mike?"

He lifted his head but seemed too frightened to speak. He pulled loose and gripped her hand. "We have to get out of here," he said with a hoarse voice.

She looked toward the area where he'd been, but she couldn't see anything that could possibly frighten him. She didn't have the courage to check it out. She held his hand and raced back across the field, past the house being built, then on to the new neighbor's yard and into their own. Mike dropped her hand and ran into the house. She caught the door before it slammed.

Inside the house, warm air wrapped around her as she pulled off her jacket and boots. Snow instantly melted on the special rug where they always set their boots to dry. Mike's boots were in the middle of the floor with his jacket in a heap beside them. Sighing, Chelsea set his boots beside hers and hung his jacket in the closet where it belonged. Mike had a lot of explaining to do!

She finally found him in the living room on the couch with the bright-colored afghan over him. He looked like he was going to suck his thumb like he had the first four years of his life.

She wanted to yell at him, but he looked so little and so frightened that her anger dissolved. She sat beside him and turned so she could look at him. His blond hair stood on end, and his blue eyes sparkled with unshed tears. "What scared you so much, Mike?" she asked softly.

He shook his head. "I can't tell you."

"Mom and Dad will be home soon. Will you tell them?"

He gasped and shook his head so hard, his hair bounced. "I can't! I can't tell them! No! You can't make me!"

With a cry of alarm Chelsea pulled Mike close and held him tightly to her. He was getting her new yellow sweater wet with his tears, but she didn't care. "Please tell me what scared you. I'll help you feel better, I promise. Jesus is with you. Remember?"

His sobbing lessened, and finally he lifted his head. She gave him a tissue from a box in the end table drawer, and he blew his nose and wiped away his tears. He moved away from her and pulled the afghan up around his thin shoulders. He took a deep breath. "I saw the spot in the woods where aliens landed." He shivered. "They aren't friendly aliens— they're out to destroy Middle Lake, Michigan—all of it."

"Mike!" Chelsea stared at him in shock at such an absurd story. He didn't usually tell such wild tales.

"It's true!" He jumped to his feet, and the afghan fell around his skinny ankles. The bottoms of his jeans were wet from snow. "I knew you wouldn't believe me! But it's the truth!"

Chelsea bit back a laugh. She didn't dare laugh out loud or she'd make him feel even worse. "Sit down and tell me the whole story."

Mike shivered, but he didn't sit down. "I saw the spot where the spaceship landed and dropped off the aliens."

"Where in the world did you ever hear such a thing?"

"I saw the spot, Chel! Honest!"

"Okay . . . Okay." She held out her hand to calm him. "Then what?"

He pointed down at his feet. "It was right there! I almost stepped in it! But I jumped back just in time. If you step where the ship landed, your legs could burn right off at the knees."

Chelsea frowned. "Mike, did those eighth-grade boys who are always teasing you tell you this?"

"No." He shook his head hard again. "I would never believe them."

Chelsea wanted to grab him and shake the whole story out, but she forced back her impatience. "Who did tell you, Mike?"

"Colin."

"Colin? Who's he?"

"A boy I met in the woods. He was there investigating. He said he was scared, but he had to check out the place so he could see how much longer before Middle Lake was destroyed."

"Mike, he was teasing you."

"No, he wasn't! He was serious. He meant every word he said! He was so scared, he could barely move."

"Did he tell his parents?"

Mike shook his head. "He doesn't dare. The aliens get real mad if you tell adults about them."

"That's silly!"

Mike's eyes snapped with sudden anger. "It is not!"

"I want to meet Colin. Would he still be in the woods?"

"He might be."

16

"Let's go see him."

"No way! I'm not going into those woods again." Mike sat on the couch and huddled inside the afghan.

"Where does Colin live?"

Mike shrugged.

"Didn't you ask him?"

"No."

"Why did you go to the woods?"

"I wanted to find an acorn to use for a school project."

"Did you get it?"

Mike gasped. "I forgot it!"

"Do you want me to go get it for you?"

He caught her hand and held it tightly. "Don't go there, Chel! I don't want anything to happen to you."

She knew nothing would happen to her because what he said couldn't be true, but she didn't want him to be scared. "Mike, Jesus is with us. You don't have to be afraid."

"Please *please*, don't go to the woods! I can get an acorn somewhere else."

"Okay . . . Okay!" What could she do to help him? "Tell me about Colin."

"I don't want to talk any more, Chel. I'm tired."

Mike tired? That was impossible! He would do his gymnastics routines over and over, run to the park and back, play all day long, and never admit to being tired. Mom had to force him to go to bed at night so he'd rest. Even then he wouldn't admit he was tired. But the minute he climbed into bed, he'd fall asleep. Chelsea had never seen anyone fall asleep quicker than Mike.

Chelsea hooked her red hair behind her ears. "Want a glass of apple juice?"

"Sure."

Chelsea hurried to the kitchen with Mike on her heels. She poured juice for both of them, and they sat at the kitchen table.

Mike took a swallow of juice, then set the glass down hard. "Does that juice taste funny?"

Chelsea tasted hers. "No. It's the same as usual."

"Mine isn't. I bet the aliens put something in my glass. I could disintegrate at any minute!"

Chelsea laughed. "Cut it out, Mike. The joke's over."

Mike shivered and pushed his glass away. "It does taste strange. I don't dare drink it. I should never have told you about the aliens! Now they're punishing me."

Chelsea started to speak, then stopped when she saw the look on Mike's face. Her mouth turned bone-dry. Mike obviously believed everything he'd told her.

What if it were all true? What if . . . ?

2

The Job

Chelsea reached for Mike's glass. "I'll taste your juice to see if it's all right."

His eyes wide with fear, Mike grabbed his glass and held it close to him. "I don't want you to disintegrate too!"

"I won't. Now, give me the glass."

The phone rang, and she jumped, almost spilling the rest of her juice.

"Don't answer it," Mike whispered, his face as white as the refrigerator door.

"I have to. It might be Mom or Dad. Or someone calling to hire the *King's Kids*." *King's Kids* was a business Chelsea had started soon after they'd moved to Middle Lake, Michigan. It involved doing odd jobs for individuals and families in the community. The Best Friends had named it *King's Kids* because they all belonged to Jesus, the King of kings.

Mike moaned and covered his face with his trembling hands.

Chelsea picked up the phone at the end of the counter. "Hello."

"Hi, Chelsea. This is Ardis Robbins, Heather's mom."

Chelsea's heart sank. None of them liked baby-sitting Heather because she was sooo spoiled. But Chelsea had to be kind because *King's Kids* tried to be kind to everyone. "Hi, Mrs. Robbins. What can I do for you?"

"We're going to have a valentine party for Heather. I want to hire you to decorate and plan the games. I'd like you to shop for the decorations and anything we'll need for the games—prizes, whatever. You're free to get help too."

Chelsea pulled her notebook out of a drawer. She kept a pad of paper by each phone in the house so she could jot down the jobs, then later write them in her *King's Kids* notebook in her room. "When do you want this done?"

"You'll need to get the games and things to me by the 12th and to decorate sometime on the 13th."

Chelsea jotted the information down. "I'll check to see who'll help me. Then I'll call you back as soon as possible."

"Thank you. Please call within the next few minutes. I must leave soon to take Heather ice-skating."

"Bye for now." Chelsea hung up and immediately started to call Hannah Shigwam. None of them had had a *King's Kids* job since just after Christmas. Even planning a valentine party for Heather Robbins would excite the others.

Mike carried his juice to the sink and poured it down the drain before Chelsea could stop him.

"Mike! I wanted to taste that!"

"Now you can't!" He ran from the kitchen and on upstairs.

Chelsea wanted to follow him, but first she had to tend to *King's Kids* business. She'd try to set up a time to shop yet tonight. "Hannah . . . hi!"

"Chel! Am I glad you called! You can't believe what the twins did!"

"Hold it, Hannah." Hannah had eight-year-old identical twin sisters and a nine-year-old sister who sometimes made trouble for her. Chelsea didn't dare let Hannah get started on a story about them or she'd be on the phone for an hour. "Would you like to help decorate for Heather Robbins's valentine party? It's a *King's Kids* job."

"Sure. Tell me when and where."

Chelsea told her as quickly as she could, then hung up to call Roxie Shoulders.

Roxie answered on the first ring.

"Hi. It's Chelsea. We have a *King's Kids* job—decorating for a valentine party for Heather Robbins."

21

"Heather? Sure, I'll help."

"Thanks." Chelsea hung up and called Kathy Aber. Her foster brother Brody answered, and Chelsea's heart stood still. She'd liked Brody Vangaar for two months. But he didn't seem to notice she was anything but Kathy's best friend. "Hi, Brody." It was hard to say his name without sounding breathless. "It's Chelsea . . . Chelsea McCrea."

"Hi, Chelsea."

She sagged weakly against the counter. He'd said her name! Could she find her voice again? She licked her dry lips and managed to ask for Kathy.

"She's not here right now. Want me to tell her something?"

Chelsea felt as if every word tripped over her tongue as she told Brody about the job.

"I'll tell her and have her give you a call. See ya."

"See ya." Chelsea slowly hung up. She was shaking so badly, she couldn't call Mrs. Robbins for almost five minutes. Finally Chelsea called and accepted the job. If she hadn't known Mrs. Robbins, Chelsea would've called someone she knew and trusted to vouch for the woman. *King's Kids* never accepted jobs from someone they didn't know and trust.

Finally she was able to think again. She finished her apple juice and set the glass in the dishwasher.

"Mike!" How could she forget his problem? She ran through the house calling, "Mike! Where are you?"

He didn't answer, but she finally found him in his bedroom—in his bed with the covers pulled tight up around his chin.

Trembling, Chelsea sank to the edge of the bed. "It's over five hours until bedtime, Mike."

"I'm tired."

She touched his forehead and cheeks to see if he had a fever the way she'd seen Mom do. He was as cold as the ice on the igloo. "Mike, how can you be so sure this boy Colin told you the truth about the aliens?"

Mike shivered. "He has proof. He hid it in his room."

"What is it?"

"He wouldn't tell me."

"He's making it up," Chelsea said impatiently. "He was only trying to scare you. I'm going to find him and tell him he's a mean bully!"

Mike flung back the cover and caught her hand. "No, don't! Please, Chelsea. It'll only make things worse."

She sighed heavily. "Look, Mike, I want to help you. Will you let me?"

"Sure. Stay with me until I fall asleep. Once I'm asleep, I'll be all right. They'll think I'm harmless and will leave me alone."

She wanted to argue further, but she could tell

it wouldn't help. "Let me get some things from my room. I'll be right back."

Mike pulled the covers over his head.

A couple of minutes later Chelsea sat cross-legged on Mike's bed and filled out the job information in her book. She opened an unlined tablet of paper and sketched a few ideas for decorations for Heather's party. It was hard to concentrate with Mike's strange story and actions racing around inside her head.

She drew a heart, then absently wrote "Brody" inside it. Quickly she erased it in case Rob or Mike saw it and teased her. She and Rob were good friends as well as being brother and sister, but sometimes he teased her about boys. She didn't want to be teased about Brody. Brody might find out she liked him, and if he did, he might laugh at her.

Maybe today she'd buy a valentine for Brody and sign it, "Your secret love." She tingled all over just thinking about it.

Suddenly Mike sat up. "I can't stay in bed any longer! I'll do my routine."

"Want me to go to the basement with you?" He usually liked being by himself, but she knew today was different.

Mike nodded.

In the rec room Mike did his tumbles and flips while Chelsea worked on a math assignment.

Suddenly Mike stopped. "Watch a video with me, will you, Chel?"

"Sure." She was almost done with her homework, and she liked watching movies. Sometimes she'd even watched movies she wasn't allowed to watch. She wrinkled her nose and flushed. But no longer! She'd promised Jesus she wouldn't do that again.

The video started with soldiers marching and bombs exploding. Chelsea frowned. "What's this movie called?"

"*War of the Worlds.*"

"I heard about it in school." Chelsea snapped her book closed. "It's about creatures from Mars taking over the earth, isn't it?"

Mike nodded. "Colin loaned it to me. He said it'll help me know how possible it is."

Chelsea laughed. Mike scowled over his shoulder at her, and she bit back the laugh.

Soon Chelsea was caught up in the video because of the love story between Dr. Clayton Forrester and Sylvia Van Buren. At a scary part Mike scooted back and sat as close to Chelsea as he could get. She didn't find it as scary as he did. When it was over, he faced her squarely.

"See! It can happen!"

"But the aliens died because they couldn't survive the germs here on earth."

"Colin said the aliens have an immune system

now that makes them strong enough to survive on our planet."

"Colin has an answer for everything, doesn't he?"

"I guess so."

Smiling, Chelsea slipped her arm around Mike. "That's only a make-believe movie we just watched. It's not real."

"He's going to loan me the *Aliens* movies. He said they're more realistic."

"Mike, you know we aren't allowed to watch those movies."

"I know. But don't you see, Chel? I have to watch them to know what I'm up against."

"They are only *movies*!"

"But where do you think the writers got their ideas? From real-life happenings, that's where! Colin said so."

"Colin is wrong!"

Mike looked hopefully at Chelsea. "How do you know?"

"I just do."

"Do you have proof?"

"No, but . . ."

"Colin has proof that he's right!" Mike leaped to his feet. He punched the Eject button, then rewound the videotape in the rewinder. The whirr was loud in the quiet room.

Chelsea sighed heavily. "Mom and Dad will be home soon. I'm going upstairs."

Mike ran to her and caught her hand. "Don't say anything to Mom and Dad! I mean it!"

She saw the pleading in his eyes and finally nodded. "Oh, all right. But I think you should tell them. They can help you see how wrong Colin is."

"You wouldn't say that if you saw his proof."

"Then I want to see it. I mean it, Mike. I want to see his proof. Tell Colin that."

Mike frowned thoughtfully. Finally he nodded. "I will! Tomorrow for sure."

"You better, or I will tell Mom and Dad. You hear me, Mike?"

"He'll show you, Chelsea. Wait and see."

Chelsea walked slowly upstairs. What did Colin have that proved aliens were real? She thought of it off and on through dinner and again later when her dad drove the Best Friends to the mall to shop for valentine decorations.

Just inside the mall Hannah jabbed Chelsea in the arm. Hannah had the high cheekbones of the Ottawa Indian, straight black hair that hung past her slender shoulders, and wide black eyes. "What are you thinking about?"

Chelsea glanced around the crowded mall, then back at the Best Friends. "I can't tell you here. Later maybe."

Roxie pulled Chelsea away from the crowd

and to a quiet area between two stores. Roxie impatiently brushed back her short dark hair. "I bet I know what it is! You got a valentine from Brody, and you haven't told us."

Kathy giggled, and her blonde curls bounced with each giggle. "Did you? And I thought he liked someone else."

Chelsea's heart plunged to her feet, and thoughts of Mike and aliens flew from her head. "Who do you think Brody likes?"

Kathy flushed. "Hey, I didn't say for sure."

"Who do you think?" Chelsea gripped Kathy's wrist. "Tell me please or I will scream right here right now."

"You won't either." Kathy laughed. "You hate to embarrass yourself."

Chelsea sank against the brick wall as a swarm of people rushed past. Kathy was right. "Please, Kathy—tell me who you think he likes."

Kathy looked helplessly at Roxie and Hannah.

"You might as well tell her," Roxie said.

"I know *I'd* rather know." Hannah was thinking about Eli Shoulders and how she'd thought he'd liked her, only to learn differently. It had hurt a lot. She didn't want Chelsea to hurt that much over Brody.

Kathy took a deep breath and let it out in one gush. "Stacia King."

"She's black!"

Kathy shrugged. "Brody isn't prejudiced."

Chelsea trembled and blinked back tears. "Are you sure they aren't just good friends because they sing together with Duke?"

"I bet that's it," Roxie said quickly. She was a little prejudiced, no matter how hard she tried not to be.

Hannah patted Chelsea's back. "We came to have fun shopping for valentine stuff. Don't think about Brody and Stacia now. We'll find out as soon as we can if they like each other." Hannah liked keeping the peace.

Chelsea finally nodded. Even if she liked Brody, she couldn't go out with him until she was older. None of the Best Friends were allowed to go out with boys yet. But that didn't keep them from liking them and having fun with them at parties.

With a shaky laugh Chelsea flipped back her red hair. "Let's go shopping! I might even buy Brody a valentine. But I won't sign my name!" She giggled, and the others joined in.

Just then she caught a glimpse of an alien on a poster in a video store. She shivered and walked faster.

3

The Valentine

Chelsea walked slowly to her locker. She should hurry or she might miss the bus, but she just couldn't hurry. Today she'd heard at least four kids talk about aliens taking over the world. She'd never noticed anyone talking about aliens before, except for the kids who'd seen movies about them. One girl thought it would be exciting to have aliens invade earth, but the other students were really scared about it. What if this boy Colin was right? Chelsea shivered.

She opened her locker and stuck her books inside. She reached for her bright green jacket and spotted a red envelope on the floor of her locker. She slowly picked it up. Her name was printed on the front of the envelope in block print, so she couldn't recognize the handwriting. Her hands trembled as she opened the envelope that was sealed only at the tip of the flap. Inside was a card with hearts and flowers and lace. A tiny boy mouse peeked from behind one heart at a tiny girl mouse. Inside she read, "I wish I was brave enough to say I love you. Be my valentine." It was signed "From Someone Who Loves You" in handwriting almost impossible to read. Her pulse fluttered, and she felt weak all over. She glanced quickly around, but no one was looking her way. Who had stuck it in her locker? Was it Brody? She sucked in air. What if it was some other boy—someone who secretly liked her?

Holding back a squeal of joy, she slipped on her coat and hurried to the door. Thoughts of aliens invading the earth flew out of her head as she ran to the waiting bus. Wind flipped her hair and turned her nose cold. She gripped the card tightly to keep the wind from stealing it from her hand. Was the boy who'd given it to her watching her right this minute? She slowed to a walk just in case. She didn't want him thinking she was a little kid.

In the crowded bus that smelled like grape bubble gum and was full of noisy kids she sat down beside Hannah and Roxie. "Look," she whispered, eagerly pushing the card into Hannah's hand.

Hannah opened it, and she and Roxie read it together as the bus lurched ahead and drove out onto the street. They both giggled with their heads close to Chelsea's.

"Do you think it's from Brody?" Hannah asked

in a low voice so the kids in the seat ahead of them or just behind them couldn't hear.

"I don't know." Chelsea felt as if she'd float right through the top of the bus. "Have you seen his handwriting before?"

They shook their heads. Chelsea rubbed the card. "I'll show it to Kathy. She should know."

Hannah frowned thoughtfully. "Anyone who wouldn't sign his own name would naturally disguise his handwriting." Hannah liked solving mysteries, and she used her great brain power anytime she could.

Suddenly Chelsea had a terrible thought. "What if a girl did this just to tease me?"

"That would not be a funny joke!" Roxie snapped. She knew she'd hate to get a card from a girl when she thought it was from a boy.

Chelsea held the card close to her. "Or what if it's from a boy who hates me and he's trying to hurt me by getting my hopes up?"

"What boy doesn't like you? You have a cute Oklahoma accent and gorgeous red hair and you're nice to everyone." Hannah tapped Chelsea's card. "I don't think a boy would do this to you to be mean."

"Me neither." Her eyes narrowed, Roxie rested her finger against her chin. "I wonder if anyone saw a boy hanging around your locker. We'll ask around."

"No! That would be too embarrassing! You'd

have to tell them why you want to know." Chelsea shook her head. "Promise you won't do it."

They agreed, then talked about boys and valentines until the bus jerked to a stop just outside The Ravines.

"Are we meeting today?" Hannah asked as they waited for their turn to walk off.

"I have to watch Mike tonight." Chelsea suddenly realized she hadn't said a word to the girls about Mike's ridiculous story about Colin and aliens. She'd tell them later.

Several minutes later she stood the valentine on her desk next to her phone. "Who sent it to me? Brody?" She stroked the mice, then the signature.

Just then Mike stuck his head around the doorway. His face was white, and his hair stood on end as if he'd been rubbing it. "Ready, Chel?"

"For what?"

"To see Colin," he said impatiently.

A shiver slithered down Chelsea's spine. Did she really want to meet Colin and see his "proof"? She saw the fear in Mike's eyes, and she knew she had to go for his sake. Once and for all she had to show Mike that Colin was a fake and so was his "proof." "Sure, I'm ready." But was she really? "Where will we meet him?"

"In our backyard."

"Why there?"

"He said so. Now, come on!"

Chelsea followed Mike downstairs for their jackets and boots. They both hurried outdoors into the cold afternoon. The backyard was empty. "Where is he, Mike?"

"I don't know, but he'll be here." Mike ran into the middle of the yard, cupped his hands around his mouth, and shouted, "Colin!"

Frowning, Chelsea pushed her hands into her jacket pockets and hunched her shoulders. She should be working on valentine decorations right now, instead of looking for proof that aliens were taking over the earth. How ridiculous!

Just then a tall, thin boy about twelve years old with a wedge-shaped face and a long nose walked into the yard. His sandy blond hair was cut short, and he wasn't wearing a cap. His navy-blue jacket hung loosely on him. He eyed Chelsea, then stopped in front of Mike.

"Hi, Colin." Mike beckoned for Chelsea to come closer.

Reluctantly she walked to his side. Colin didn't look weird or strange like she figured he would, considering that he believed in aliens. Chelsea wanted to run back inside and work on valentines, but she knew she'd have to stay with Mike.

Mike gripped Chelsea's arm. "This is my sister Chelsea that I was telling you about. She's going with us."

Colin shrugged.

"Where do you live?" Chelsea asked.

"Right there." Colin pointed to the house just behind the McCreas'.

Chelsea's eyes widened in surprise, and then she frowned down at Mike. "Why didn't you say so?"

"I didn't know." Mike shrugged. "I only saw him in the trees."

"Ready?" Colin asked.

Chelsea's stomach tightened. Should she take Mike and go back inside their house?

"We're ready." Mike started across the yard, tugging Chelsea with him.

Colin ran on ahead of them to the back door and held it open for them.

Inside, Chelsea hung her coat on a hook and pulled off her boots as Mike and Colin did the same. The house was warm and very quiet. It smelled like furniture polish. She was ready to follow Colin upstairs, but instead he led the way down the hall and into his bedroom. The McCreas used that room as the study in their house. The computer on his desk looked like Rob's. His bed was covered with a blue blanket but no bedspread. White mini-blinds hung at the windows instead of curtains. A TV with a VCR stood in one corner on a wooden stand. The walls were bare. The room was clean and orderly, but somehow it didn't feel lived in.

Mike moved closer to Chelsea. "Where is it, Colin?" Mike asked just above a whisper.

Colin looked suspiciously at Chelsea. "I know you don't believe anything I've told Mike."

"No, I don't." Chelsea slipped an arm around Mike. "I'm not stupid, you know."

"I know." Looking deadly serious, Colin bent down and reached under his bed. He pulled out a cardboard box that once had held cans of tomato soup, then tapped the top of it. "The proof is right in here. I found it in the trees where the spaceship landed. I don't know if it fell from inside the ship or off the landing gear."

Chelsea frowned. What a fake!

Mike trembled and looked ready to cry.

Colin tugged at the neckline of his gray sweatshirt. "The night we moved in, I saw the spaceship land. I sneaked out of the house and ran to the spot. The ship was gone, but I could see the marks where it had landed. And I found this . . . I put it in this box we'd had stuff packed in." He tapped the box again. "It's a piece of strange metal—part aluminum, part plastic, and part something I can't identify." He started to open the lid, then stopped. "I watched a video that showed documented accounts of spaceships landing. On one of them they told about this very piece I have here."

Mike pressed close to Chelsea.

She swallowed hard. Colin seemed very, very sure of himself. But what he was saying was impossible! "Just show us," she said impatiently.

"This is real," Colin said softly. "We must believe what's happening or we'll be taken over before we know it. We'll be slaves to people from another planet."

"You've been watching too many outer space movies." Chelsea forced a laugh, but it sounded forced, and she flushed with embarrassment.

"I do watch them . . . so I can learn all I need to know." Colin brushed his hand over his face. His nose looked extra-large as he frowned. "Before we moved here, I belonged to a group of people who knew aliens would someday try to take over the earth. I learned what to watch out for." Colin sighed heavily and looked very unhappy. "My folks decided to move here after Christmas—I think they wanted to get me away from my friends. But it doesn't matter. I know what I know. Besides, I'll soon have a group here who will help me stand guard."

Chelsea felt a chill deep inside her. "Just show us the thing, will you?"

"I will! But I want you to understand first."

"I understand," Mike whispered.

Colin nodded. "I know you do, Mike."

"I came to prove to Mike you're a fraud!" Chelsea snapped. This was getting to be too much. She didn't want to admit it, but she was starting to think Colin might be telling the truth because he sounded and looked so sincere. She couldn't let him convince her that aliens were taking over the world!

Colin took a deep breath. "I have to tell you what happened next before I can show you." His face ashen, he trembled and cleared his throat. "It was the most frightening thing that ever happened to me."

Chelsea's skin prickled with fear. She tightened her arm around Mike and felt him tremble.

Colin tugged the neck of his sweatshirt again. "It happened three days after I found this." He touched the box. "I was asleep. Sound asleep. Sometimes I have a hard time sleeping because I am worried about what's going to happen." He swallowed hard. "An alien visited me during the middle of the night."

Mike cried out and buried his face against Chelsea's arm.

She shivered. "No! You're making that up."

Colin shook his head. "It's real. Honest, it is! He woke me up. I don't know how, but he did, and he said if I told any adult about what I'd found he'd see that my folks were killed."

"Killed!" Chelsea cried in horror.

Mike burst into tears. "I told you, Chelsea! Didn't I tell you?"

Colin brushed at his eyes as if he were trying not to cry. "I begged him not to hurt my mom and dad. He said he wouldn't as long as I kept my word and didn't tell any adults. So I didn't tell anyone but Mike. Now I'm telling you. But you both have to promise not to tell an adult."

"I promise," Mike said quickly. "So does Chelsea. Right, Chel?"

She shrugged. She felt like she had a boulder in her stomach. "Let me see what's in there."

Colin slowly opened the lid. He hesitated, then lifted out what looked like a piece off a car.

Chelsea laughed, suddenly relieved. "It's just part of an old car."

"No, it's not," Colin said patiently, as if she were a baby. "No car is made with these materials. Don't you think I already checked that out? Believe me, I wanted it to be a part of a car. But it's not."

"Did you show it to someone?"

"Yes. A mechanic. Of course I didn't tell him what I thought it was or where I got it. I just showed him so he could tell me if it came off a car. He said it didn't." Colin held it out to Mike. "Want to touch it?"

Mike jumped back. "No!"

Chelsea shivered. She didn't either.

Colin put the thing back in the box, closed the lid, and slid the box back under his bed. He sank to the edge of the bed. "I need help. I can't stop the aliens by myself. Will you help me?"

Chelsea frowned. "What can we do? We're just kids."

Colin lifted his chin, and his hazel eyes flashed. "There's no time to be just kids! We have to take the responsibility of overpowering the aliens!" He lowered his voice. "Or make friends with them if we can't make them leave here."

"I still don't believe you." Chelsea shook her head while Mike huddled against her.

Colin ran to his VCR and clicked out a tape. "Take this home and watch it. Then you'll believe me."

Chelsea stuck her hand behind her back. "I don't want it!"

"Because you're afraid you'll believe me, right?"

"No!" Chelsea grabbed the tape. "Oh, all right, I'll watch it. But not for my sake—for Mike's. It's not good for him to believe such nonsense."

Mike shivered.

Colin pushed his hands deep into the pockets of his jeans. "I wish I didn't believe it. But somebody has to know the truth."

"Did you ever see *War of the Worlds*?" Chelsea asked sharply, knowing he had, but curious what he would say about it.

Colin nodded. "The aliens that have invaded us are not like those. They can tolerate our atmosphere. Some say they can even take on human form."

Mike moaned.

"I don't believe it," Chelsea said angrily.

"I don't know if I do either, but I'm keeping an open mind. You should do the same. It might keep your family from being destroyed."

Chelsea's head spun with all that she'd heard. She had to get out of there fast. "Come on, Mike." She faced Colin. "I'll watch the video and get it back to you tomorrow. But don't count on me believing any of this."

Colin barely moved his head. "I already know you'll believe it, Chelsea McCrea. I knew it the minute I saw you."

Her stomach in knots, Chelsea pulled Mike with her out of Colin's bedroom. She didn't even glance toward the bed where the box was hidden.

4

The Long Night

Chelsea stood in front of the big-screen TV with the video from Colin in her hand. Should she or shouldn't she watch it? Was it all right for Mike to see it? He was barely nine, not twelve like she was.

"Do it, Chel!" Mike jabbed her arm. "Before Mom gets home."

Chelsea reluctantly clicked in the tape. Mom was working part-time the next few weeks at the newspaper office. She usually got home just after 5, and Dad a few minutes later.

Mike sank cross-legged to the floor. "Sit with me, Chel."

She sat beside him as the video started with a flicker. It showed a spaceship zooming to earth. She gasped. This was a home video! Had someone set this all up just to fool others, or was it for real?

"I told you," Mike whispered hoarsely.

"I still don't believe it," she snapped. But she

watched as the police came and then the military. She listened to the woman who'd first spotted the ship tell the camera all that she'd seen before she'd had a chance to grab her video camera. The video ended with military officers telling all the people who'd seen the strange object that it was only a missile from the Armed Forces, not from outer space. They took it away and refused to speak further of it. Later that night the woman had a visit from a strange creature looking for his ship. She only told about it and couldn't show it because she'd been too terrified to get her video camera. She said it had thin arms and a large head with a wrinkled forehead. It wore a uniform that looked much like aluminum foil.

The video ended, but Chelsea couldn't move. Could it be possible?

"I told you," Mike whispered. He jumped up, his face white and his eyes wide in fear. "I told you. Now maybe you'll believe me and Colin. Maybe now you'll help us stop the takeover!"

Chelsea popped out the tape and pushed it into its case. "Mike, I still don't believe it. If it were true, others would know and would be working at stopping them."

He shook his finger at the TV. "You saw what the military said! They lied! They don't want mass hysteria, so they say there is no life on other planets and that we don't have anything to fear. You saw the truth with your own eyes!"

"Mike, Mike . . ." Chelsea saw the terror Mike was feeling, and she reached for him.

He jumped away. "Don't try to talk me out of it! I know what I know."

Before Chelsea could answer, she heard Mom shouting to them. She stuck the video under a pile of games in a closet where neither Mom nor Dad would see it.

Mike stood on the stairs and wouldn't let Chelsea pass. "You won't tell Mom and Dad, will you?"

She hesitated, then shook her head. "I won't." Why had she said that? She should tell them so they could help Mike. But what if Colin was right and she caused her parents to be killed? She shuddered.

Slowly Mike walked upstairs. Frowning, Chelsea watched him. She couldn't remember Mike ever walking up the steps. He usually *ran* up and down. Actually he ran everywhere he went, unless he did flips to get to his destination. This was really hard on Mike. He was suffering, really suffering. She'd have to do everything she could to make him feel better.

Later Chelsea sat in her room with the Best Friends. Red and white poster paper and lacy doilies lay scattered around them. It was hard for Chelsea to get in the mood to work on decorations.

Kathy looked at the valentine Chelsea had found in her locker. "I wonder if Brody did give you this."

Chelsea frowned. "What?"

Kathy held up the valentine. "This."

"Oh, that."

The Best Friends looked at Chelsea in surprise. "What's wrong?" Hannah asked in concern.

Chelsea laid down the scissors she was using and looked at the Best Friends thoughtfully. She could tell them what Colin had said since they weren't adults. They'd probably laugh at her, but she had to know what they thought. "What do you think about aliens taking over the world?"

As Kathy and Roxie laughed, Hannah peered closely at Chelsea. "Are you joking?"

Chelsea forced a laugh. "I guess. I just wondered if you girls ever thought about aliens taking over the world . . . Or trying to."

Roxie smoothed the lacy heart she'd been working on. "Last year some kids in my class got really scared about that when they saw a movie about aliens. Dad wouldn't let us see the movie, but the kids at school who did see it said it was realistic, and they thought it could happen. One girl—Sarah James—was so afraid she missed several days of school."

Chelsea's mouth suddenly felt bone-dry. "What made her get over her fear?"

"Her mom talked to her."

Hannah touched Chelsea's arm. "Are you afraid, Chelsea?"

She managed to laugh. "Me? Did I say I was?"

"No, but you're acting strange."

Chelsea ducked her head. Hannah sometimes saw too much! "If aliens did take over, what would we do?"

Kathy giggled. "I'd make friends with them."

Chelsea looked sharply at her. "What if they didn't want to be friends?"

Kathy shrugged. "It wouldn't matter. It's not going to happen."

"We have angels watching over us," Hannah said with great assurance. "God says His angels are watching over us to keep us safe. Personally, I think angels would have more power than any alien—if there is such a thing—which I doubt."

Chelsea breathed a sigh of relief. Yes, she did have angels watching over her! She didn't need to be afraid. Why hadn't she thought of that before? She smiled and picked up the paper beside her. "I guess we'd better get some more things made."

Kathy cut a heart out, then held it as she said, "I heard about a woman, Peggy Hart, who was really really tired because she had several kids, all of them too young to help. She was tired of washing diapers and cooking meals. This was a long time ago, before disposable diapers and frozen dinners.

Peggy Hart was so tired, she was crying and praying for help. A woman came to her door and said, 'A friend sent me to cook and clean and watch the children for you today so you can rest.' Later Peggy Hart learned the woman was an angel in disguise!"

Roxie pulled her knees up to her chin. "Dad said he read about a man who was buried alive in a cave-in while he was working construction. The man asked God to send an angel to help him. Just like that, the man felt like he could breathe, and he stopped being afraid. A long time later they dug him out of the cave-in, and he was perfectly all right. The doctor said it was a miracle that he lived that long under the heavy dirt. The man said an angel protected him."

Hannah flipped back her long dark hair. "In the Bible Daniel was tossed down in the lions' den, and God sent an angel to shut the lions' mouths so they couldn't eat Daniel. I know angels are real."

Chelsea breathed a sigh of relief. The girls were right—angels *were* real. She didn't have to be afraid of aliens. Smiling, she picked up the valentine she'd found in her locker. "Kathy, do you think Brody gave this to me?"

"It's possible. He has terrible handwriting, but I can't tell for sure if that's his."

"I wish I had the courage to ask him." Chelsea rubbed her finger over the sprawled signature.

They talked about getting and giving valentines

as they worked on the decorations for Ardis Robbins. Chelsea decided she'd get one for Brody for sure.

She smiled as she thought about slipping it into his locker. Would he guess that it came from her?

Much later Chelsea climbed into bed and yawned. The light from the hall brightened her room enough to see the pile of decorations on her desk and the special valentine sitting on the night-stand beside her bed. Was it from Brody?

Yawning again, she closed her eyes. Immediately pictures of aliens flashed across her mind. Gasping, she opened her eyes and stared wide-eyed up at her ceiling. She glanced at her door that she'd left open a crack. Maybe she should open it wider. She frowned. She wasn't a baby! She would stop thinking about aliens!

Music drifted in from Rob's room. He always fell asleep with his gospel music playing. Mom and Dad were downstairs talking about their day as they did every night. They usually didn't come to bed until after the news.

Just then the bedroom door opened, and Chelsea sat bolt upright, her heart racing. Wearing a T-shirt and pajama bottoms, Mike walked in, and she sighed in relief. "Mike, why aren't you asleep?" He was always asleep by 9:30.

Sniffing back tears, he leaned against her bed. "I can't sleep. I keep thinking about aliens."

Chelsea slipped out of bed. Her Oklahoma nightshirt hung to her knees. She took Mike's hand. "Come on. I'll tuck you back in bed and stay with you until you're asleep."

"Thanks, Chel." He clung to her like he had when he was little and they were shopping at the mall.

In his room she pulled the covers back and watched as he climbed into bed. He looked so little as he laid his head on his pillow. She covered him, then sat on the edge of his bed. "Mike, you have angels watching over you all the time. They're big and strong."

"Would they keep the aliens away?"

"Aliens aren't real."

With a cry he sat up. "Chel, you know they are! You saw the video and Colin's proof, and you heard all that Colin told us."

She nodded. "Shhh." She patted his shoulder gently. "Don't think about aliens now. Think about angels."

Mike settled back down and closed his eyes. "Angels will watch over me."

"That's right."

Mike suddenly burst into tears. He sat up and flung himself into Chelsea's arms. He pushed his face into her neck. "I keep seeing those aliens on the poster."

Frowning, she looked around. He had pictures

of gymnasts on one wall and baby seals on another wall. "What poster?"

"In my desk. Colin gave it to me."

Chelsea pulled away from Mike and opened his desk drawer. She found the poster tucked between two books on gymnastics. She shivered as she looked at the horrible figures. The aliens looked like some she'd seen on "Star Trek: The Next Generation" on TV, only even uglier and scarier. "I'm going to throw this away."

"No!" Mike lunged for it and pulled it out of her hands before she could wad it up. "Colin said I have to keep it so I'll never forget."

Chelsea sighed. "Then put it back in the drawer and get to bed."

Mike looked at the alien, then slipped the poster back into the drawer. He looked at Chelsea as if he were going to cry again. "Do you think the aliens will kill Mom and Dad while we sleep tonight?"

"Mike! No!" Chelsea's nerves tightened. But what if the aliens did come and kill them during the night? She pushed the horrible thought aside. "Get into bed, Mike. I'll sit right here until you're asleep."

Mike slowly climbed into bed. He lay with his eyes wide open, his body tense.

Chelsea sat beside him. She remembered that when Mike was little, she'd rub his head so he'd sleep. She reached out and gently stroked his head.

"Tomorrow we'll check out the igloo to see how it's holding up. We can sit inside and tell stories if you want." Chelsea talked about maybe building an igloo themselves and how they'd do it. Finally Mike relaxed and closed his eyes. Before long he fell asleep. Chelsea leaned over and kissed his cheek. "Sleep tight, Mike."

Sighing tiredly, Chelsea walked slowly to her room. She absently ran her hand over the tall red letters that spelled *Oklahoma* on her nightshirt. Had anyone back in Oklahoma ever thought about aliens taking over the world?

In her room she left her door open wide as she slid between the sheets. Rob's music clicked off, leaving a great silence. She stared up at the ceiling until she heard Mom and Dad walk up the stairs. She closed her eyes. She heard them stop at Mike's door, Rob's, and hers to check on them just as they did each night, then walk to their room.

With a sigh Chelsea turned on her side and closed her eyes. She fell asleep and dreamed about aliens swarming all through the house. They killed Mom and Dad, Mike, then Rob, and were coming after her. In her dream she screamed and ran, but no matter how fast she ran, they ran faster. They caught her in the rec room and held up the videotape she'd hidden there. Slowly they came after her, surrounded her, and caught her. They smelled like decaying trash and felt rough like a piece of dried toast.

She woke abruptly, her skin damp with sweat. She clamped her hand over her mouth to hold back a scream. "It was only a dream," she whispered, "only a dream." But it was a long time before she could get the images out of her mind.

As she lay there she heard sobs coming from Mike's room. Wearily she slipped out of bed and crept down the hall. He was sitting up in bed, with tears streaming down his ashen face. She couldn't remember a time when he hadn't awakened early with a shout and a smile. She sat on his bed and pulled him close to her. "Shhhh. It's all right, Mike. I'm here."

But was it all right? Would it ever be all right again?

5

The Long Day

Chelsea wearily pulled on some jeans and the first sweater she found. It was a blue one with pink and mauve flowers across the front of it. Her grandma had sent it to her for her twelfth birthday, December 29. Usually it took her fifteen minutes just to decide what sweater to wear, then fifteen minutes more to brush her hair and fix it just right. But this morning she'd overslept, so she had to hurry. She brushed her hair quickly, pulled it back into a ponytail, and looped it with a blue band. She heard Mom calling Mike again.

Mom stuck her head inside Chelsea's room. Mom's shoulder-length red hair hung down on her slender shoulders. She wore a plaid western shirt and Levis. She frowned slightly. "I can't understand why you two overslept this morning. Is something wrong?"

Chelsea wanted to blurt out about the aliens

and Mike's fear, but she forced back her words just in case Colin was right. "Will you be home today when we get off the bus?"

"No, so I'll need you to watch Mike again."

Chelsea's heart lurched. She couldn't face Colin and his alarming talk again today! "Why can't Rob do it?"

Mom looked at Chelsea in surprise. "He's working. You know that. Is something wrong, honey?"

"Should there be?" Chelsea dramatically flung out her hands. "I always have to baby-sit Mike when I want to do something else. I can't understand why I always have to watch Mike! It's not fair! You're the mother! You should be watching him!" Even as she said the sharp, wounding words she wanted to grab them back, but they were out there between herself and her mom. They'd done their damage, and it was too late to stop them.

Mom peered into Chelsea's face. "Something is wrong! What is it?"

Chelsea spotted the valentine on her nightstand, and that gave her an idea. "Somebody sent me a card, and I don't know who."

Mom read the card and smiled. "How sweet! You don't have to worry about this, honey."

"I don't?" Chelsea hugged Mom tight. "I'm sorry for what I said. I really don't mind watching Mike."

"I know you don't." Mom patted Chelsea's back, then kissed her cheek. "I knew something besides the baby-sitting made you upset. It is hard to get a valentine from a boy and not know who sent it. I remember one time when I was thirteen a boy sent me a card. I was really scared because I thought it was from a boy I couldn't stand. But it wasn't. It was from the boy I liked. Colin Aspinn was his name."

Chelsea froze. Colin! Just hearing the name brought all Chelsea's agony back, even though Mom's Colin wasn't the boy she and Mike knew. "I have to hurry, Mom."

"I know. I'll have to drive you and Mike to school. That'll give you time to eat breakfast." Mom rushed to Mike's room, calling to him to hurry too.

Chelsea sank weakly onto her chair. This was the first time she'd ever missed the bus. What would Hannah and Roxie think? It was even too late to call them to tell them. What would she tell them when they asked why she'd overslept? They'd laugh at her if she told them she was beginning to believe aliens were taking over the world. She frowned. Then she remembered that they were her best friends—they wouldn't laugh! She'd tell them when she could sit down quietly and relate the whole story without interruptions.

Later in math class Chelsea opened her math book so she could hand in her assignment, then sank low in her seat. The paper was gone! She must have left it home in her pack. Reluctantly Chelsea raised her hand.

"Yes, Chelsea." With her long earrings dangling almost to the shoulders of her red sweater, Mrs. Williams leaned against her desk.

Chelsea's face burned with embarrassment. It felt like a million eyes were on her. "I left my paper at home. Could I hand it in tomorrow instead?"

Mrs. Williams sighed, then nodded. "But have a parent sign it, so I'll know you didn't wait and do it today."

"I will."

"Do problem 9 on the board for us."

Chelsea gasped. "Me?"

The class laughed as Mrs. Williams nodded.

Slowly Chelsea walked to the board at the front of the room, her book in her hand. The students laughed even harder. Why were they laughing? She knew she had on jeans and a sweater that went together okay. She could understand if she'd accidentally worn her Oklahoma nightshirt to class.

At the board she turned and spotted Hannah a few seats back. Chelsea caught Hannah's eye, and Hannah motioned to Chelsea's shoes. She looked down only to discover she had a hightop Nike on one foot and a lowtop Reebok on the other. Her face flamed, and she couldn't remember one thing about math. Helplessly she turned to Mrs. Williams. "May I be excused, please?"

Mrs. Williams slipped her arm around Chelsea. "Don't worry about having on different sneakers. Once I wore my old ragged slippers to school and didn't know it until the day was half over. No one bothered to tell me. I couldn't figure out why people were laughing when I walked past. You may take your seat."

Chelsea thankfully sat down. How could she have put on different sneakers?

After class the Best Friends swarmed around her desk, and all three asked at once, "Chelsea, what's wrong?"

"I'll tell you when we meet tonight," she whispered. They stayed in the same room for their next class—science, so the girls sat down again. Chelsea opened her science book to try to read the assigned pages before the class began. Suddenly she remembered they were having a chapter quiz. The color drained from her face, and she sank low in her desk. Was she going to fail a quiz? That had never happened before—never! What would Mom and Dad say?

Later Mrs. Williams passed out the quiz, and Chelsea quickly looked it over. Silently she asked the Lord to help her. She knew some of the answers. Maybe it wouldn't be as bad as she'd thought. But actually it turned out worse. She failed the test and had only four correct answers.

Just after lunch she heard two boys in the hall talking about aliens, so she left the Best Friends and walked boldly up to the boys. "Hi, Troy. Hi, John."

They looked at her questioningly. "Hi," they both said.

She cleared her throat. "I didn't mean to listen in, but I heard you talking about aliens. I've been . . . uh, wondering about them lately." She lowered her voice. "Do you guys think they're real, or were you just talking about a movie you saw?"

Troy ran a finger around the inside of his collar as if it was too tight. "I think they're real, but I can't prove it."

John nodded. "I had a funny dream that didn't really seem like a dream last night—like an alien came to my room looking for something."

Chelsea trembled. "Do you know Colin?" Chelsea searched her memory for his last name, then realized she'd never heard it. "I don't know his last name, but he just moved to Middle Lake several days ago. He lives at The Ravines."

"I don't know him," John said.

"Me neither." Troy frowned. "Why?"

She told them as quickly as she could. "But I think the thing he has as proof is only a part of a car. I don't believe what he says."

"You should," Troy said sharply. "I heard my

dad talking to a couple of his friends. They said we'll be taken over for sure before the end of this year."

Chelsea groaned. The bell rang, and she had to rush to class. So Colin wasn't the only one who believed aliens were going to take over the world! Could the aliens really take control of the human race by the end of the year? Chelsea shivered.

At home after school Chelsea quickly pulled off her good sweater and slipped on a gold sweatshirt. She'd accidentally worn old jeans to school, so she left them on. She changed into matching sneakers, then ran downstairs. Her stomach ached with hunger, but she knew she wouldn't be able to swallow a thing until she returned the video to Colin.

Mike stood at the back door with the video in his hand, his jacket and boots already on. He had dark circles under his eyes. "Hurry up, Chelsea!"

"I'm coming." She pulled on her jacket and hurried out after Mike.

Colin was waiting in their backyard. He took the video from Mike and thrust another one into Chelsea's hand. "Watch this one to learn how to fight the aliens when the time comes."

She looked down at it and knew it was a video her parents had forbade her and the boys to watch. "I can't watch it."

"You have to, for your own safety!" Colin sounded frantic. "And for the safety of your family—of the *world*!"

Chelsea sighed. "All right. But Mike can't watch it. I'll tell him what he needs to know from it."

Colin nodded.

"I want to see the thing you found again," Mike said.

Colin shook his head. "My dad is home, so you can't come over. He'd ask you all kinds of questions, and you might slip and tell him why you came to see me. I don't dare take that chance. He thinks I've given up the theory that aliens are out to destroy us. For his own sake I don't want him to know differently."

Chelsea bit back a sigh of relief. She didn't want to go to Colin's ever again. She thought of the talk in school with Troy and John. "Colin, what's your last name?"

"Mayhew. Why?"

"I was telling a couple of boys in school about you. They want to get together with you." Chelsea frowned. "How come you don't go to school?"

"I do . . . A private school."

"Oh. How come?"

Colin shrugged. "My mom wants the best for me. My dad says he doesn't want my brain to atrophy. He's against public schooling."

"Do you believe in angels?" Mike asked suddenly, looking closely at Colin.

"Angels?" Colin furrowed his brow. "Angels?"

Chelsea nodded. "You know . . . Angels. God created them."

"I heard stories about them and saw pictures of them, but it never occurred to me to think they were real."

"They are." Chelsea turned up her jacket collar against the stinging wind. They couldn't invite Colin inside because no one was allowed over when Mom and Dad were gone. "We know angels are real, and we know they would be stronger than aliens."

Colin shook his head. "That's impossible."

Mike stepped close to Chelsea.

She put an arm around Mike. "It's true. Angels protect us. They would protect us from aliens if they came."

"I don't think so. Aliens have all this high technology that angels wouldn't have." Colin looked off toward the woods. "I was going to check the trees again in case another spacecraft landed."

"I'll go with you." Mike sounded scared but determined.

"I don't know," Chelsea said.

"I'll see that he gets back home safely." Colin started across the yard with Mike beside him.

"Be home before Mom gets here, Mike."

"I will." Mike lifted his hand in a wave, then ran off with Colin.

Chelsea slowly walked inside and took off her

jacket. She looked down at the video. Should she watch it? She'd always wanted to see it, but hadn't because Mom and Dad had said it was too violent. She had promised herself she would never watch another video she wasn't supposed to watch, but this was different. She had to see it, so she'd know what Colin meant about fighting off the aliens.

In the rec room she pushed the video into the VCR and sat back to watch it. Maybe it wasn't wise to watch it all alone, but she couldn't very well have anyone with her either.

At the first scary part she hugged a cushion extra-close to her and tried not to scream. At the second scary part she screamed before she could stop herself. Her whole insides trembled with fear. Just at the most frightening spot, when it looked like the aliens were winning, Mom called downstairs.

Frantically Chelsea clicked off the video and hid it in the closet. She was trembling with fear because of what she'd seen—and because Mom had come home early.

Chelsea took a deep breath and ran upstairs. Mom was in the kitchen drinking a glass of apple juice. "You're early," Chelsea said in as normal a voice as she could manage.

Mom nodded. "I finished early, so I asked if I could leave. I wanted to be home with you and Mike." She frowned. "Where is Mike?"

Chelsea's heart zoomed to her feet. She licked

her dry lips as she tried to think of the best thing to say. "We met the new neighbor boy—his name is Colin Mayhew—and Mike went with him to explore the woods. He'll be back soon."

"How old is Colin?"

"My age, maybe a little older."

"I suppose it's all right then." Mom finished her juice and put her glass in the dishwasher. "I'll go change, and then we can start dinner."

Chelsea nodded. She felt weak all over, but she didn't move until Mom walked out of the kitchen. Then she sagged against the counter and let her breath out in one loud *whoosh*. The video she'd watched flashed into her mind. How had it ended? Somehow she just had to see the rest of it. She couldn't stand not seeing the end of a movie or reading the end of a book.

In the video would the aliens win or lose? In real life would they win or lose?

She walked to a kitchen chair and sank down weakly.

6

Dad's Questions

Chelsea heard the back door close, and she raced from the kitchen to talk to Mike. He looked ready to fall over in a dead faint. "Mike, Mom's home already, so be careful of what you say."

He slowly took off his jacket and boots and dropped them in a heap. "I'm going to bed."

Chelsea caught his arm. "What happened?"

Mike's eyes filled with tears. "Colin found evidence of another visit from aliens." Mike brushed at his eyes. "I can't talk anymore. Let me go to sleep."

"Mom will wonder why you want to hit the sack so early."

Mike sank to the floor. "I'm so weak, I can't walk."

With shivers racing down her spine, Chelsea helped him up. Had an alien done something to Mike to make him sick? "You have to act like everything's all right, Mike. You don't want Mom to ask you questions, do you?"

Mike struggled to stop crying. "What will we do without a mom and dad?" he whispered tearfully.

"Nothing will happen to them!" Chelsea sounded surer than she felt.

Mike stood up and leaned against Chelsea. "Did you watch the video?"

"Most of it."

"Did you learn anything?"

"I guess." She frowned. What *had* she learned? She couldn't go running all over the country killing off aliens, especially if she couldn't recognize them. "Come in the kitchen for a glass of apple juice. It'll make you feel better."

Mike reluctantly walked with her and drank a glass of juice. Mike usually ate a peanut butter and jelly sandwich before dinner just so he could survive until mealtime. He didn't want one today.

At dinner Chelsea watched Mike pick at his food. He liked fried chicken breast strips, mashed potatoes, buttered carrots, and tossed salad. But this time he ate only one chicken strip and two bites of potatoes. He ate a small piece of carrot just because Mom asked if he was all right.

As they ate, Rob talked excitedly about the skating party they were going to Saturday afternoon. He was a year older than Chelsea and had curly auburn hair. When they'd lived in Oklahoma he'd stayed at his computer night and day, but now he had a part-time job and actually did things with others. He still enjoyed his computer, but it wasn't his entire life. "I've never skated on a pond before," he said even though everyone knew it. They'd all learned at an indoor ice rink. Mike was the best at it.

Chelsea had totally forgotten about the skating party. Stacia King's grandma had hired the Best Friends to plan the surprise ice-skating party for Stacia. Roxie had sent out invitations, Hannah had bought the hot chocolate and marshmallows for afterwards, Kathy had taken Stacia ice-skating several times just so she'd know how before the party (Stacia had caught on very quickly), and Chelsea had seen that everyone had a ride to and from the pond at the nearby park. Everything was all taken care of. Now she just had to remember to attend.

Dad pushed his plate back and leaned his elbows on the table. He narrowed his blue eyes and stroked his mustache the way he always did when he was deep in thought. "All right, gang, what's going on?"

Chelsea froze. She didn't look at Mike, but she felt his tension.

"Nothing's wrong, Dad," Rob said in surprise.

Dad tapped Chelsea's arm. "Hun bun, what's wrong?"

Chelsea opened her eyes real wide and tried to look innocent. "Nothing that I know about." It wasn't a lie because she didn't know if aliens really were taking over the world.

"Mike?" Dad asked softly. "I've never seen you leave the table without eating everything, maybe even your napkin! You haven't eaten more than five bites."

"He overslept this morning too," Mom said in concern.

"Mike did? That settles it. Now I know something's going on. Out with it, Mike."

He looked helplessly at Chelsea, but she didn't know how to help him out.

Dad frowned. "Mike?"

He gulped a great gulp of air. "There's a kid at school who keeps trying to fight with me."

Chelsea almost cried out. Mike never told a lie! But he'd lied just now.

"Who is it?" Mom asked sharply. "I'll go right to school tomorrow and put an end to it!"

Bursting into tears, Mike leaped up. "No, Mom! Please don't do that. I can take care of myself. I'm not a baby!"

Dad walked over to Mike and lifted him high in his arms, then sat back down with Mike on his knee. "Mom won't go to school, but if this continues, we'll call your teacher and talk about how to deal with the situation."

Mike knuckled away his tears. "I'll be all right."

Chelsea's stomach ached so badly, she thought she'd have to excuse herself from the table. She forced herself to sit still so she wouldn't bring attention to herself. She'd have a talk with Mike later. He knew it was a sin to lie!

After dinner she finally found Mike alone in his room. He was sitting on his bed looking sad. "Why did you lie to Mom and Dad?" she hissed. She didn't want Rob to hear.

Great tears welled up in Mike's eyes. "I couldn't help it. I couldn't tell them the truth! The aliens would kill them."

"Oh, Mike . . ." Chelsea sat on the bed with him and held him tight.

Just then she heard the Best Friends coming upstairs to see her. She kissed Mike and stepped into the hall. "Hi," she said, barely able to hold back her tears.

They all said hello, and then Kathy said, "I can't stay long. I have to watch Megan tonight." Megan was four and sometimes had an imaginary friend.

"Then we'll get right to the decorations." Chelsea listlessly motioned to the pile of papers on her desk. Making valentine decorations didn't seem important at all, but she had to keep working as if she were still interested in doing it. "I think we'll have them finished tonight, so I can take them to Mrs. Robbins after school tomorrow. Saturday is the skating party." Chelsea could barely keep her mind on what she was saying.

"Tomorrow after school we're supposed to go to the mall to get the rest of our valentines," Roxie said as she cut out a heart.

Chelsea frowned. "We are?"

The Best Friends stared in surprise at Chelsea, and then they all talked at once. The words seemed to pound against Chelsea. Tears rose up inside her and spilled from her eyes. She covered her face and sobbed in intense sobs that shook her entire body.

"What's wrong with her?" Roxie whispered to Hannah and Kathy.

They shrugged. Hannah put an arm around Chelsea and leaned her head against Chelsea's. Kathy patted Chelsea's knee. Roxie pushed aside the decorations and slid closer to Chelsea. They sat silently praying for Chelsea until she stopped crying. They knew sometimes the best thing was to sit quietly and wait.

Finally Chelsea blew her nose and wiped her eyes and cheeks dry. Haltingly she told them all about Mike and Colin and aliens taking over the world. She even told them about watching the terrible video that she'd been forbidden to watch. "And Colin really believes everything he's told us about aliens!"

Before anyone could say anything, the phone rang. Chelsea jumped up to answer it, her head pounding from crying so hard. It was Hannah's mom saying she had to come right home.

"I'm sooo sorry I have to leave now. We'll talk again as soon as possible," Hannah said, hugging Chelsea tightly.

Chelsea nodded.

Kathy glanced at her watch and jumped up. "I have to go right now too!" She hurried out after Hannah.

Roxie walked to Chelsea's window and looked out a long time. Finally she turned to Chelsea. "I heard some kids talking to Eli about aliens." Eli was Roxie's sixteen-year-old brother.

Chelsea laced her fingers together. She didn't know if she wanted to hear what Roxie was going to say.

"They said there's life on other planets. They said aliens could take over the world if they wanted to." Roxie shivered. "I'd like to talk to Colin and see what he has in that box. I'd like to be ready if aliens are going to invade us."

Chelsea moaned. She hadn't wanted Roxie to want to meet Colin. "You could meet him tomorrow after school."

"We're going to the mall."

"Oh. I forgot."

"How could you forget? You want to buy Brody a valentine."

"I forgot."

Roxie gasped in surprise. "Chelsea, something is wrong with you if you forgot about buying a valentine for Brody. If you don't like him anymore, tell me." Roxie licked her lips and cleared her throat. "I like him too."

Chelsea stared at Roxie in shock. "How can you like him when I do? What kind of friend are you?"

Roxie lifted her chin high. "I said if you don't like him anymore, I will! Why are you getting so mad at me?"

Chelsea tried to calm down, but she couldn't stop the flow of angry words. "You're always trying to take a boy away! You tried with Kathy, and now you're trying with me! I can't believe you're doing this to me! Don't you dare call yourself my best friend!"

Roxie's face darkened with anger. "I won't! And don't you dare call yourself my best friend!" Roxie ran from the room and down the stairs.

Chelsea slammed her door shut and flung herself across the bed. She played the argument over and over in her mind. How could Roxie dare like Brody?

Just then Mike opened the door and walked in.

"I'm going to watch the video tonight after Mom and Dad are asleep. Will you watch with me?"

"You can't watch it, Mike," Chelsea snapped.

"I'm going to, and you can't stop me!"

Chelsea stared at him in shock. Was that her little brother? Finally she nodded. "I better watch with you. It's too awful to watch alone."

Just before midnight Chelsea and Mike crept guiltily to the basement and clicked on the lamp and pushed in the video. Mike moved as close to Chelsea as he could get. She knew he shouldn't watch the video, but she didn't stop him. She was too tired to argue.

She tensed as the first scary part was coming up. She didn't want him to see the spurting blood and the frantic fighting between the humans and the aliens. "Cover your eyes, Mike. Here comes a really really bad part."

"I am going to watch all of it, no matter how scared I get!"

She sighed heavily, but let him watch. When the scary part came, he gasped and trembled. At the next part he covered his mouth and screamed a muffled scream.

Just then the overhead light clicked on, and someone ran down the steps. Chelsea and Mike leaped up and turned, their eyes wide in alarm. Frowning, Dad walked toward them, wearing his bathrobe and slippers. The video seemed to get even louder behind them.

"What is going on here?" he asked sharply. He looked at them, then at the TV.

Mike ducked behind Chelsea and pushed his face into her back. She shivered and couldn't find her voice.

Dad strode to the TV and shut off the video. The silence seemed deafening. He was quiet a long time.

Chelsea peeked through her long lashes at him. He looked as if he couldn't believe she'd disobey him. The pain in his eyes made her want to cry as hard as Mike was.

Dad cleared his throat. "I am surprised to find you both up this late and watching a movie you weren't allowed to watch. Chelsea?"

She hung her head, but she couldn't speak around the hard lump in her throat.

"Mike?"

He whimpered but couldn't say anything.

"It's too late to talk now, so get up to bed. Tomorrow when I get home from work we'll have a long talk. Then I'll tell you your punishment. I'm too upset to deal fairly with you now."

Mike sank to the floor in tears. Dad picked him up and motioned for Chelsea to go ahead of him. She slowly walked up the steps, her legs cast-iron heavy.

At her bedroom door Dad said, "Good night, Chelsea. I love you."

She crept into her bed and buried her face in her pillow. What was happening to her? Her life was falling apart. But it really didn't matter since aliens were going to take over the world anyway.

7

Brody

Surrounded by the noise of lockers banging and students laughing and talking all around her, Chelsea leaned against her locker and wished she'd been able to stay home from school like Mike had. She would've liked to have Mom baby her all day like she was going to do with Mike. Chelsea trembled. Would Mike break down and tell all about Colin and the aliens? He better not, just in case what Colin had said was true! It would be awful to be without Mom and Dad.

Fear stung her skin, and Chelsea tried to pray, but she couldn't form the words in her mouth or in her mind. Her heart felt as frozen as the snow outdoors.

Just then Hannah walked up to Chelsea. Hannah's arms were full of books, and she looked upset. "Chel, why is Roxie so mad at you?"

"Mad at me?" Chelsea pulled her books out and slammed her locker with a loud bang.

"She says you're mad at her, and she won't tell me what it's about." Hannah pushed back her hair as she fell into step with Chelsea. "We agreed that as best friends we'd always talk things out instead of being mad at each other."

Chelsea finally remembered about her fight with Roxie. Anger rushed through her again. "Roxie is no longer my friend!"

"Don't say that!" Hannah stopped short directly in front of Chelsea, so she stopped too.

Chelsea's head throbbed, and her eyes burned from being tired. "Nothing you can say will change my mind."

Tears sparkled in Hannah's eyes. "You can't break up the Best Friends! What would we do without Roxie?"

"Don't do without her. Drop *me*." Chelsea ducked around Hannah and hurried toward class. Her head swam with what the world would be like if they were slaves of aliens. Best friends wouldn't count then.

At the door Brody Vangaar stopped her. He had dark hair and eyes and wore a red pullover shirt and jeans. He smiled hesitantly. "Did you get it?"

Chelsea frowned. What was he talking about? "Get what?"

Brody flushed and looked around quickly. "The valentine I pushed into your locker," he whispered.

Chelsea shrugged. "Oh, that. I got it." She started past him.

"I thought . . . I thought you wanted me to give you one," he said in a low, tight voice.

Her head was too full of Mike and Colin and aliens and Dad to think about Brody. "I can't talk now." She brushed past him and walked into class. As she sat down she realized she'd actually been rude to Brody Vangaar, the boy she'd loved for weeks now! What was wrong with her?

Frantically she ran back out into the hall to look for Brody. He was probably already in the seventh grade part of the school. What had she done?

Kathy hurried to Chelsea's side. "Is something wrong?"

"Brody . . . He told me he sent me the valentine, and I didn't say I was glad or anything!"

Kathy patted Chelsea's arm. "You have to come back to class. The tardy bell rang. Mrs. Williams gave me permission to come get you."

Chelsea moaned and helplessly shook her head. "What'll I do now? He'll never talk to me again. He won't skate with me at the party or anything!"

"Shhhh. Don't cry. Come to class now before you get in trouble with Mrs. Williams." Kathy tugged gently on Chelsea's arm.

Slowly Chelsea walked back inside the classroom. She didn't have the energy to struggle or even talk. She saw John and Troy, the boys who also believed aliens were going to take over the world, and immediately she stopped thinking about Brody and started worrying about the future of her family.

The day dragged on even more than the last day of school. Chelsea refused to sit with the Best Friends at lunch or on the bus going home. She had to clear her mind so she could deal with Dad tonight.

After school she walked from the bus alone. She saw Hannah and her sisters stop at the igloo and touch it to see how it was holding up. Chelsea kept on walking. She didn't care if the igloo collapsed today. She knew it wouldn't because it was still too cold, but nothing was important except seeing Mike and Colin to find out what was going to happen next.

She walked into her house as quietly as she could. The smell of popcorn swirled around her, but it didn't make her mouth water as usual. She heard Rob talking to Mom in the kitchen. Chelsea's stomach tightened. What would Mom say about last night? She and Dad had probably talked about what they'd say at the terrible meeting tonight. They always decided together what punishment to give.

Chelsea hung up her jacket and slipped off her sneakers. Maybe she'd be grounded until she was twenty-one! She hurried upstairs to Mike's room. It was empty but clean. How could she find out what was going on if she couldn't speak to Mike in private?

Sighing, she hurried to her room. She stopped short just inside. Mike was sitting in the middle of her bed, looking as frightened as he had last night.

"I've been waiting for you," he said with a catch in his voice.

Chelsea's mouth turned as dry as cotton. "What did you tell Mom?"

"Nothing."

"Did you talk to Dad at all?"

"He called at his lunchtime and asked me how I was feeling. I said fine." Mike slipped off the bed and gripped Chelsea's hand. "But I'm not fine at all! I went to get the video, and it was gone!"

"Dad probably took it."

"I know! I couldn't ask Mom about it." Mike shivered. "What if he finds out it's Colin's?"

Chelsea gasped. "How could he?"

"I don't know. I do know Dad met Colin's dad a few days ago."

Chelsea sank to her chair. "We have to talk to Colin."

"I tried to call him this afternoon."

Chelsea grabbed the phone. "He should be home now. What's his number?"

Mike pointed to numbers scrawled on a piece of scrap paper taken from the hearts she'd been making.

Chelsea quickly punched the numbers. Colin

answered on the first ring. "This is Chelsea. Can you talk?"

Mike pushed his head close to Chelsea's so he could listen.

"Yes. I'm home alone. You sound scared."

"We're in big trouble!" She quickly told Colin what had happened. "Our dad is really upset."

"No problem. Tell him a neighbor kid loaned you the video, and you didn't know it was going to be that bad."

Chelsea's eyes widened. "We can't lie to him!"

"Oh, all right. Try this then—tell him you're really sorry and will never do it again. Tell him you were both curious about aliens, so you wanted to see it to learn more about them. Stay calm, and act like you're really sorry."

"We *are* sorry!"

"You'll be thankful you saw it once you have to do actual battle with the aliens."

"We didn't see all of it," Mike said.

"Watch the rest before you return it."

"We can't." Chelsea tightened her hold on the phone. "We think Dad has it."

"Tell him it belongs to me. He can yell at me if he wants. I don't mind."

"I guess we better hang up," Chelsea said tiredly.

"Wait! I want to meet those two boys you told

me about—John and Troy. Set up a meeting, will you?"

"They're going to an ice-skating party Saturday afternoon at one o'clock at the park. Be there, and I'll introduce you to them."

"I'll be there."

Chelsea hung up, then just sat there with her head in her hands and her elbows on her desk. The phone rang, and she almost jumped through the ceiling. She answered it in a tiny voice.

"Chel, it's Hannah. Meet us out front right away. Mom's taking us to the mall."

"To the mall?"

"For valentines. Chelsea? You didn't forget, did you?"

"I guess I did. I really don't want to go."

"But you want to buy a card for Brody, remember?"

Chelsea sagged back in her chair. "I forgot. I'll be right out." She hung up and started for the door.

"What about me?" Mike wailed. "Are you leaving me here all alone?"

"Mom's here."

"I want you here!"

"Cut it out, Mike. You're not a baby, you know."

Mike burst into tears.

Chelsea scowled at him and ran downstairs.

She poked her head into the kitchen. Mom sat at the table with a cup of tea and a book. "Hi, Mom."

She looked up and smiled at Chelsea. "Hi. Want some popcorn?"

"No thanks. I'm going to the mall with Hannah to get the rest of the valentines. Is that okay?" Chelsea held her breath and waited.

Mom nodded. "Be back for dinner."

"I will." Chelsea hurried away. She knew after tonight's talk she could very well be grounded, but for now she wasn't.

Hannah's mom was waiting in her station wagon at the curb. Chelsea slipped into the warm car just as Roxie ran from her house. Chelsea frowned. "I'm not going after all," Chelsea whispered.

Hannah caught her arm. "Please do. Please *please*!"

Chelsea sighed and gave in. "But I won't talk to Roxie. I mean it!"

Roxie slipped into the car, smiled, and said a cheery hello.

Chelsea stared at her in surprise. Why wasn't Roxie still angry at her? She'd said she'd stay mad.

At the mall the Best Friends walked through the entrance near Penney's. Roxie caught Chelsea's arm. "I want to talk to you."

Chelsea tried to jerk free, but Roxie's grip was too tight. Kathy and Hannah walked on ahead, then stood looking in the window of a clothing store.

"I told them to leave us alone for a while," Roxie said.

"Don't say a word to me," Chelsea snapped.

Roxie smiled. "I was wrong to get mad at you and yell at you. I'm sorry. I've decided that even if you are mad at me, I won't be mad at you. I'm going to be nice to you no matter how you treat me. That's what Jesus wants."

Chelsea couldn't say a word as she stared at Roxie, who'd been a Christian a shorter time than the rest of them. She usually had a hard time doing what Jesus said.

Roxie laughed. "Let's go buy valentines, shall we? You buy one for Brody. I'm not going to—even if you don't."

Tears pricked Chelsea's eyes, but she wouldn't let them fall. Life had been so simple when she and the Best Friends had done ordinary things together. Now everything was different. And all because of aliens!

8

A Serious Talk

Listlessly Chelsea pushed the valentine she'd bought for Brody into her desk drawer. It wasn't important. Nothing was, except the talk that was coming up in a few minutes. She heard Mike crying in his room. He was afraid he'd break down and tell the truth. He couldn't stand thinking he would be to blame for their family being destroyed. Rob had gone to a friend's house until 9, so his music wasn't playing as usual.

Chelsea touched her phone. Should she call Hannah and tell her what had happened last night? She hadn't said a word about it to the Best Friends while they were shopping. They'd been so excited about choosing just the right valentines that she couldn't find a way to say anything.

Trembling, she turned away from the phone and looked at her watch. It was time to meet Mom and Dad in the study. Chelsea's stomach knotted painfully. Slowly she walked to Mike's room. "It's time."

Bravely he dried his eyes and stopped crying. His lower lip quivered as he looked pleadingly up at her. "Don't let me tell about the aliens, Chel. Please!"

"I won't." But could she stop him if he started talking? Somehow she had to.

Downstairs she stopped outside the study. She heard the soft hum of voices and knew Mom and Dad were already there. The smell of chocolate still hung in the air from the brownies Mom had made for dessert. Chelsea hadn't been able to eat even one bite because of the terrible ache in her stomach. She knew Mike hadn't either.

Chelsea pushed the door all the way open and walked in with Mike on her heels. Mom sat in a red leather chair, while Dad leaned against his desk. They both smiled. Chelsea couldn't smile back. She looked down at the gray carpet with her hands locked together in front of her. Her blue sweater suddenly felt very hot.

Mike moved until he touched Chelsea.

"Sit down, kids." Dad hiked himself up on his desk and crossed his ankles. His black socks matched his black dress pants that he'd worn to work. His white shirt was open at the neck, and he'd taken off his tie.

Chelsea perched on the edge of the couch, and

Mike sat as close to her as he could. Chelsea couldn't push even one word through her tight throat. Mike didn't say anything either.

Mom crossed her legs and picked at a string on the seam of her jeans.

Dad brushed a finger over his mustache. "Kids, your mom and I have been talking and praying about the right words to say and the right way to handle this situation."

Chelsea squirmed uneasily.

Mom leaned forward slightly. "We know it's not like you children to disobey the way you did last night. We know something serious is going on."

Chelsea's nerves tightened. This was going to be different than she'd thought. They were not just going to lecture a few minutes, then tell the punishment. She heard Mike whimper.

"Mike, you've turned into a bundle of nerves," Dad said in a voice full of concern. "You don't eat or sleep, and I never see you do your gymnastics anymore."

"I'll start eating, I promise! I'll sleep too, and I'll practice all day long." Mike sounded desperate.

"Easy, Mike," Mom said softly. "We aren't going to force you to do anything."

Chelsea slipped her arm around Mike. She felt him relax a little. She tried to relax too but couldn't.

Dad cleared his throat. "In this house God is

the head of the family. He knows everything about us. He knows what's been going on with you kids."

Chelsea could barely breathe. She'd forgotten about that.

"And He wants to help you with every problem you might have—no matter how big the problem, or how small." Dad rested his hands on either side of him. "I've never seen the video you kids were watching, but I've heard about it. My assistant Sharon talked about it for days. She was afraid aliens were going to take over the world. She thought I'd laugh at her when she told me, but I didn't. I never laugh at things that frighten people, no matter how they sound."

Chelsea hung on every word Dad was saying. Maybe he'd say something that would help them.

Dad smiled. "I told Sharon I believed in angels. I said angels are sent to guard us and help us, and even if aliens are real, we still don't have anything to fear. God is with us, and all His angels are with us. How can a mere alien defeat God's own creation? It's impossible."

Hope fluttered inside Chelsea.

"I don't believe there is life on other planets," Mom said. "But it doesn't matter what I believe about aliens. I can't prove or disprove life on other planets. But I can prove through God's Word that nothing can destroy us. Satan came to kill, steal, and destroy us. But Jesus came to give us abundant life!

Jesus defeated Satan, so all we have to do is resist the Devil and tell him to get away from us in Jesus' name, and he must obey."

"That's right," Dad said, smiling. "Nothing and no one is more powerful than God." Dad looked very serious. "But Satan can make you think something is stronger or has more power. Satan is a liar and a deceiver. Jesus is truth. He will never leave you. And His strength is yours. No aliens—if they are out there at all—can destroy you or me, because Jesus keeps us safe. We are protected always! The Bible says that no weapon formed against us will prosper. That means that we'll be victorious no matter what weapon is used against us."

Mike jumped up and ran to Dad. "Dad, can an alien kill you?"

Chelsea held her breath and waited for the answer.

"No, Mike," Dad said firmly.

"Or Mom?"

"No, Mike." Dad slipped off his desk and knelt beside Mike. "We have God's protection on us, just as you and Chelsea and Rob have on you."

Mike flung his arms around Dad's neck and held on tight.

Chelsea's eyes filled with tears.

Mom walked to the couch, sat beside Chelsea, and slipped an arm around her. "God is our Father. He watches out for us all the time."

Chelsea clung to Mom's hand. "If aliens have already invaded the earth, would we still be safe?"

Mom nodded. "Yes. But I don't believe it has happened, no matter what others say. I believe Satan uses movies like the one you kids watched to make people afraid. If Satan can put fear in your heart, he can destroy your happiness and even your life."

Chelsea knew her happiness had been destroyed for sure.

Dad sat in the chair and pulled Mike onto his knees. "God's Word says that as a man thinks in his heart, so is he. If you'll dwell on God's words, you'll be worry-free and able to do good things. If you think on scary stuff, you'll always be afraid. Whatever you think about, talk about, read about, or watch on video or TV will rule your life. We in this house are Christians. The Bible assures us that we have not been given a spirt of fear but rather power and love and a sound mind—that means self-control. But Satan wants to trick us into giving in to fear." Dad patted Mike's leg. "That's why we won't let you watch the wrong kind of movies or read the wrong kind of books. We don't want you to fill your minds with destructive things. We want you to fill your mind with God. We want you to have a spirit of love and power and a sound mind." Dad looked questioningly at Mike, then over at Chelsea. "What do you two have on your minds that has been hurting you?"

"Aliens," they both said at once. They no longer wanted to keep the secret, especially now that they knew Mom and Dad were safe.

Mom gently pushed Chelsea's hair off her cheek. "How did that happen?"

Chelsea glanced at Mike, then at Mom. "The new neighbor boy says aliens are going to take over the world and make us slaves."

"He has proof," Mike broke in.

Dad hugged Mike close. "No matter what proof he has, God is stronger. God is our protection."

"That's right." Mom nodded.

A great weight had lifted off Chelsea, and it felt sooo good. "I wish I'd talked to you about it earlier! Why didn't I tell you what was scaring us?"

"Because Satan is a deceiver and a liar," Dad said. "You believed a lie." Dad shook his finger. "But no longer! Your mom and I prayed for you both last night and all day today. We knew we'd get to the bottom of this. We knew we weren't just dealing with disobedience. And praise God, He answered our prayer!"

Tears slipped down Chelsea's cheeks as she and Mike took turns telling about Colin and his stories about aliens.

"We didn't want you to be killed," Mike said with his arm around Dad's neck.

"That's nice of you, but once again Satan used that lie to hurt you and us. If you would've told us right off about this alien thing, we could've told you we're safe." Dad pulled Mike to his feet, then pushed himself up. He walked to Mom and Chelsea with his hand held out to them. "We're going to pray together now for us and for Colin. We're going to do everything we can to help him know that Jesus loves him and wants him to be free of his terrible fears."

Mom and Chelsea and Dad and Mike stood in a circle holding hands while Dad prayed.

Chelsea whispered, "Forgive me, Jesus, for disobeying You and for forgetting that You're here to help me. I'm sooo sorry!" While Dad prayed, she prayed silently for Colin and even for Troy and John. Aliens or not, they didn't have to be afraid.

Several minutes later Dad said, "Is the video Colin's?"

Mike nodded, and Chelsea said, "Yes. We're sorry we watched it."

"So are we," Mom said.

"We've prayed it won't cause you nightmares or any more fear." Dad held up the video. "I'd like to destroy it, but I can't because it belongs to Colin. I will have a talk with that young man, though. It's not healthy for him to dwell on such things."

"Colin doesn't have Jesus as his personal Savior," Chelsea said. "We'll tell him about Jesus."

Mike nodded. "Maybe then he'll have something else to talk about and think about."

Mom smiled and agreed, and then they talked some more.

Chelsea wanted to twirl around the room and shout for joy. She was free of agony! The room was full of love instead of tension. How wonderful it felt!

Several minutes later Mom tapped Mike on the head. "There's time for a snack before bedtime if you're interested."

"Yes!" Mike flipped on his hands with his feet high in the air and his back arched. He walked on his hands to the door.

Chelsea laughed as they followed Mike to the kitchen. It was good to see the old Mike back. She couldn't wait to tell the Best Friends about their special talk with Mom and Dad tonight. Suddenly she thought about Roxie. She had to call Roxie and tell her she was sorry. As soon as she went to her room, she would. But first she wanted to have something to eat. It seemed like it had been forever since she'd enjoyed eating and talking with her family.

She and Mom peered into the refrigerator and finally decided on leftover lasagna. While it was heating in the microwave, Chelsea made garlic toast with melted mozzarella cheese on top for everyone. The kitchen soon filled with mouth-watering aromas.

Chelsea glanced at Mike just as he looked at her. They smiled, then laughed right out loud.

9

Best Friends Again

Laughing, Chelsea ran across the backyard with Mike beside her. She knew that if the yard weren't covered with snow, Mike would be doing handsprings and flips.

His cheeks and nose red with cold, Mike laughed up at Chelsea. "Colin's sure gonna be glad to know he doesn't have to be afraid of aliens taking over."

"He sure will!"

A minute later Chelsea knocked on the back door of Colin's house. She couldn't wait to tell Colin the great news. Somewhere down the street a dog barked. She heard a snowmobile roaring in the distance.

"Answer the door, Colin!" Mike ducked around Chelsea and knocked on the door. "Maybe Colin's in the woods."

"Maybe." Chelsea waited a little longer, then

ran across the open space, past the house being built, and into the woods. Birds flew from the trees. A squirrel ran to the end of a branch and scolded loudly. Chelsea cupped her hands around her mouth and shouted, "Colin! Are you here?"

Mike shouted for their friend too. "Colin, it's Mike and Chelsea! We want to talk to you."

They stood quietly and waited for an answering yell, but when none came they walked into the woods to the place where Colin had found the strange indentation where he was sure a spaceship had landed. Chelsea looked at the sunken ground without a shiver of fear.

Mike stood at the edge. "Do I dare step in?"

Chelsea laughed. "Sure, why not?"

"Yeah, why not?" Mike stuck his toe in. He looked at Chelsea, then walked right into the area and giggled. "My legs didn't disintegrate like Colin said they would!" Shouting happily, Mike jumped all over the sunken area. "I'm not scared any longer! I wasn't given a spirit of fear—the Devil is a liar—Jesus is the truth!"

Chelsea laughed. "We were given a spirit of power and love and a sound mind! Yes, we were!" She leaped high and twirled around. She landed in the snow and skidded, then threw out her arms for balance. It felt wonderful to be free of fear! "Let's go, Mike. Colin isn't here. We'll see him later."

"I sure wish he'd been here." Mike touched his

legs below his knees. "He was positive my legs would turn to ashes from the knees down."

"Well, he was wrong!"

Mike jumped up and down and shouted, "Wrong, wrong, wrong!"

Chelsea laughed, feeling as lighthearted as Mike.

After dinner Chelsea was still smiling as she met with the Best Friends in her bedroom. She waited until they were sitting down on the floor around the decorations, then said, "I have an important announcement to make."

They looked up at her. "What?"

"I am no longer angry at Roxie." Chelsea bent down to Roxie. "I wanted to call you last night, but it was too late when I finally got the chance." Chelsea smiled. "I'm sorry for being so mean to you. Please forgive me."

Roxie squeezed Chelsea's hand. "I already did."

"Thanks."

"I'm sure glad you're you again." Roxie raised a dark brow questioningly. "What happened to make you change your mind?"

"I finally saw what I was doing." Chelsea sank down in the circle facing Roxie. One knee touched Kathy's and the other Hannah's. "Now, for the rest of my story. You all are gonna love it!" With a lot of interruptions she told them about the talk with

Mom and Dad last night and the outcome of it. "We tried to take the video back to Colin just after school, but he wasn't home."

"I'd like to meet Colin," Roxie said.

"You will, at the ice-skating party tomorrow." Chelsea told them about Colin planning to attend just to meet John and Troy. "They're all sure aliens are going to take over the world. Colin's going to show the boys his proof that they exist."

"Proof! There has to be a logical explanation. I am going to solve the alien mystery." Hannah sounded very determined. "We know a spaceship didn't land in those woods. How ridiculous!"

Kathy tapped her chest with her open hand. "I am going to see that Colin gets out on the pond to skate tomorrow at the party. It sounds like he needs attention from kids his age who aren't into aliens."

Chelsea laughed with the others. "I say let's make Colin Mayhew a Best Friends' good deed! Who votes yes?"

"I do!" they all said at once, then giggled.

While they finished the decorations for the party for Heather Robbins, they talked about what they would do for Colin.

Smiling, Kathy leaned back with a faraway look on her face. "My very favorite valentine party was when I was six. Mom planned it all just for me—not for Duke. He didn't like parties. Megan wasn't born yet, of course. So the party was only mine. I wore a red and white dress with little red shoes. Five other girls came, and we played with our dolls, then ate little sandwiches, a heart-shaped cake, and ice cream with red punch. I wanted to keep the dress forever." Kathy sighed. "Mom gave it away. She said we should let another little girl enjoy it."

Hannah twisted the tip of her braid around her finger. "When I was ten I wanted a birthday party so badly . . . But I didn't have any friends. Mom decided to have a party for me anyway. The twins and Lena were the guests, and they came to the door and rang the bell just like real guests would've. They each carried a gift for me, and they were dressed for a party. We played games and ate, and I opened my gifts. It was great."

Roxie wrinkled her nose. "My worst party was when Mom invited boys when I only wanted girls to come. The boys didn't have fun at all. Two of them didn't even bring gifts! That was the worst part for me. I like opening presents. Now I'd like to have a party with both boys and girls. My birthday is March 2, and I want to invite all of you to my party. Now we have to decide which boys to ask."

Chelsea laughed. "Unless your mom won't let you have boys."

"She will. I already asked her. I just wonder who I should ask."

"Brody for sure," Chelsea said. "And Rob because he kind of likes you, Roxie."

She gasped. "Your brother likes me? I didn't know that!"

"He says he likes your sense of humor, and he thinks it's great that you can carve little animals like you do."

"But does he really like me—you know, for a girlfriend?"

Chelsea didn't want to lie. "I don't know. All I know is what I've already said."

"Then I'll invite him. Duke too. It would be terrible to invite Brody and leave Duke out."

"He would be hurt," Kathy said.

Chelsea absently stacked the hearts they'd cut out. "Once in Oklahoma a neighbor boy, Steve, had a birthday party and asked Rob but not me. He'd asked both boys and girls, but he was mad at me because I hit a home run at a game we'd had at the park." Chelsea rolled her eyes. "Can I help it if I'm good at softball? Anyway, I tried to sneak into the party so I could at least have cake and ice cream, but Steve caught me and made me leave."

"What a jerk," Hannah snapped, then flushed. "Sorry. But that *was* wrong of him!"

"It sure was! But I forgave him and even taught him how to hit a ball. He learned quick." Chelsea giggled. "He didn't want anyone to know I was teaching him, so he practiced extra-hard."

Chelsea jumped up. "Time to go! We've got to get these things to Mrs. Robbins. I hope it's not snowing since we have to walk." Mrs. Robbins lived several houses away.

"We don't mind walking in the snow." Kathy playfully tugged Chelsea's hair. "But we don't have Oklahoma blood that turns cold at the first sign of a snowflake either."

The girls laughed as they gathered all the decorations up and hurried downstairs. Chelsea told her mom where they were going. "We shouldn't be long."

Chelsea's mom turned from the stove where she was boiling water for a cup of tea. "Tell Ardis Robbins I do have the heart-shaped baking pan she asked me about."

"I will. I could take it to her and if she doesn't want it, bring it back."

"Good idea." Mom pulled the pan from the shelf and handed it to Chelsea.

Chelsea stuck it in the bag of decorations. "We might try to see Colin before we come back in."

"Your dad said he spoke to Colin's dad this morning. Colin and his mother are gone until late tomorrow morning."

"Okay. Too bad." Chelsea was really anxious to tell Colin he didn't have to be afraid any longer, but it would have to wait until tomorrow.

Several minutes later Chelsea rang the doorbell at the Robbins family's house, then huddled deep into her coat. It wasn't snowing, but it was cold enough that she could see her breath.

Ardis Robbins opened the door. Her dark hair was pulled back with a wide red ribbon. She wore jeans and a red and black sweater. She looked like a grown-up version of Heather. "Hi, girls! I was beginning to wonder if you'd get the decorations here before Heather got home. Come in."

Chelsea gladly stepped inside and moved so the others could come in. Then she pulled out the baking pan. "Mom said you can use this if you want."

"Thank you. I will bake a heart cake. Heather should like that, don't you girls think so?"

They nodded. Chelsea knew Heather would expect the ultimate. It was very hard to please Heather. She was used to getting her own way about *everything*.

Ardis looked in the bag and frowned nervously. "I don't know if I can handle the actual party. I can put up the decorations and get the food ready, but . . ." She looked pleadingly at the Best Friends. "Could you girls please come over Sunday afternoon and be in charge of the party? You know more about what kinds of games to play and how to get the kids excited about them than I do."

Chelsea's heart sank. She really didn't want to be at Heather's party, but she didn't want to hurt Mrs. Robbins by saying no. Chelsea looked at the girls to see what they'd say.

Roxie shrugged. "Sure, we'll be here." Roxie got along better with Heather than any of them.

Ardis sighed in relief. "I'll be very thankful for the help. And I'm sure Heather will enjoy herself more with you girls here." Ardis looked at Hannah and flushed. "I hope your little sisters don't feel badly about not being invited."

Hannah had a hard time talking around the lump in her throat. "They think they're invited. They said Heather told them they were, so they're planning on coming."

"Oh dear." Ardis twisted her hands nervously.

Chelsea moved closer to Hannah to try to comfort her.

Hannah was sure her sisters weren't welcome just because they were Ottawa Indian. "What should I tell them?" she asked in a low voice.

Ardis sighed heavily. "Heather's two cousins are coming, and their mothers, my husband's sisters, are very prejudiced."

Chelsea lifted her chin. "We won't help at the party then."

"That's right," Roxie and Kathy said.

Ardis gasped. "But I can't manage on my own."

"Couldn't you explain to your sisters-in-law that Heather wanted all her friends to attend and that included the Shigwam girls?" Chelsea wanted

101

to say a whole lot more, but she knew it wouldn't be right.

Ardis finally nodded. "I suppose I can. The girls are welcome to come—as long as you girls will be here to help."

"We'll be here," Chelsea said firmly.

A few minutes later the girls walked slowly back toward Chelsea's house. They didn't say anything about what had happened.

"Thanks, girls," Hannah finally said.

"What are best friends for?" they all said at once, then laughed.

Chelsea's heart swelled with pride to know she could be a part of the Best Friends. If her mind had been full of fear of aliens taking over, she'd have missed the special feeling they were all having by helping Hannah. Silently she prayed, *Jesus, thank You for giving me victory over fear.*

The Ice-skating Party

Chelsea's heart leaped with excitement as she watched Stacia King walking across the park toward the skating pond where all the kids were waiting to yell, "Surprise." Stacia thought she was just coming to skate with Kathy. A bonfire burned nearby where they could get warm, sending the smell of wood smoke high into the air.

"She is going to be sooo surprised," Kathy whispered with a low laugh.

"It's a perfect day for skating." Hannah looked at the bright sun, then at the smooth ice.

Roxie glanced around, then tugged on Chelsea's arm. "Is Colin here?"

"I don't see him." Chelsea looked around, then turned back to watch Stacia. Her long, frizzy black hair bounced as she walked. Her eyes glowed in her beautiful brown face. Chelsea remembered that when Stacia had first come to live with her grandparents at The Ravines she'd hated everything and everybody. She'd missed her family a lot, but couldn't live with them because of the dangerous school she went to. Now she liked going to school at Middle Lake Middle School, and she had lots of friends. She was one of the best singers Chelsea had ever heard. Often she sang at birthday parties with Brody and Duke. Today Brody and Duke had brought their guitars, so later Stacia would sing for everyone—at least that's what they had planned.

As Stacia reached the spot they'd marked ahead of time they all shouted, "Surprise, Stacia! Surprise!"

She stopped short, her hand over her heart. "What's going on?"

Chelsea ran up to Stacia. "Your grandma and grandpa wanted to throw a party for you, so here it is!"

Tears welled up in Stacia's eyes. "I can't believe it! This is fantastic!" She touched Chelsea's arm. "You and your friends did this, didn't you?"

"Yes. It was fun. Come on, get your skates on and skate!" Chelsea ran with Stacia to the bench near the ice.

Soon Chelsea glided out on the ice and joined several others already skating. She caught a glimpse of John and Troy, then searched the crowd for Colin. Finally she spotted him standing at the edge of the pond, his skates in his hand.

Chelsea skated quickly to the Best Friends and pointed Colin out to them. They had a plan worked out to make sure Colin had a good time. Roxie was to be the first to approach him.

He saw her coming, and his stomach tightened. He wanted to run away from the whole laughing crowd, but he wanted even more to meet John and Troy so he could set up a new network here in Middle Lake.

Roxie stopped beside Colin. "Hi. I'm Roxie."

"I'm Colin."

"I'm a friend of Chelsea's. Come skate with me, will you?"

"Sure . . . Okay." Colin wanted to refuse but wasn't sure what to say. So he sat on the bench and quickly tied on his skates.

Roxie sat beside him. "I live right next door to Chelsea. I have an older sister Lacy, a little sister Faye, and a brother Eli—he got his driver's license not long ago. Do you have any brothers or sisters?"

"No." A few years ago he'd wanted a brother so badly, he'd cried himself to sleep every night. But now that he knew about the horrible danger from aliens, he was thankful he didn't have a brother.

"My dad's a contractor. How about yours?"

"He works at Benson Electronics."

"So does Chelsea's dad! Did you know that?"

"No." Colin wanted Roxie to leave him alone. He walked awkwardly to the ice, then stepped out onto it. Once he'd been a great skater, but during the last two years he'd been too caught up with getting ready for the aliens to do anything else.

Roxie caught Colin's hand. "Let's go!" She laughed and skated smoothly across the ice. She knew he wanted to find Chelsea or Mike, but she wanted to get his mind off aliens for a while. "Isn't it a perfect day?"

Colin hadn't noticed, but he looked up at the bright sun and across the ice at the laughing skaters. A hard knot tightened in his stomach. They had nothing to laugh at, but they didn't know that. He had to warn them about the takeover! He knew he couldn't shout a warning. He'd tried that once in school. The teacher had sent him to the office, and the students had made fun of him from then on.

Abruptly Colin pulled free of Roxie. "I have to find Chelsea right now!"

Roxie motioned quickly to Kathy, and she whizzed over to them. "Colin, this is Kathy, another friend of Chelsea's. Go with her."

"Hi, Colin." Smiling, Kathy caught his hand and skated away with him. "I'm glad to meet you. I live outside The Ravines, not far from here. In the summer I always bring my little sister Megan to play here at the park. I have two brothers—Duke and Brody. They play guitar. Do you?"

Colin shook his head. It had been so long since

he'd talked about anything but the coming invasion that it was hard to follow a regular conversation.

"See the African-American girl skating there? She's Stacia King, and this party is for her." They skated around a couple of kids who'd fallen on the ice. "She sings with my brothers. She's going to sing after a while. I think you'll like it. What kind of music do you like? I love listening to Amy Grant!"

Colin's head was spinning faster than the boy ahead of them, who was spinning so fast he was a blur of color. Suddenly the boy came to a stop, and Colin saw it was Mike McCrea. "I have to talk to Mike."

Kathy was prepared for that. She laughed and whirled around, pulling Colin with her. She stopped beside Hannah. "Colin, this is Hannah. She's Chelsea's friend too, and she lives right across the street from her."

Hannah smiled. "I have a huge stone in my front yard."

Colin was immediately interested. He'd wondered about the boulder. "Where did it come from?" he asked as he skated away with Hannah.

Hannah's black hair flowed out behind her as they skated around a group of girls who were practicing spins. "When the basement of our house was dug, they came across that huge stone. They were going to carry it away, but Mom wanted it as a yard decoration." Hannah giggled. "It's easy to give directions to our house. We tell them we're the only ones on the street with a giant rock in our front yard."

"I used to collect rocks," Colin said. He'd forgotten about that until just now. Then he frowned. Rock collecting was for someone who didn't know the immediate danger from outer space.

"My dad used to too. He has some labeled and hanging in a frame on the wall in our family room. You're welcome to come look at them."

Colin almost accepted, then shook his head. "I don't have time."

"Have you seen the igloo? It's right next door to us. See the girl in the yellow jacket over there? That's Alyson Griggs. The igloo is at her house. Actually we share it because we all helped build it. You're welcome to crawl in it anytime you want."

He had wanted to crawl into the igloo just to see how it felt inside, but he hadn't done it. He'd always had too many important things to do. Frantically he looked around. "I came here to meet two boys, John and Troy. I don't know their last names, but Chelsea was going to introduce us."

"Sure, I know them. They play basketball on the middle school team."

Colin frowned. "They do?" How could they do anything so frivolous when the world was in danger? Maybe they wouldn't be the help he'd thought.

Just then Hannah stopped beside Stacia. "Stacia, this is Colin. He's new at The Ravines."

"Hi, Colin. Want to skate?" Stacia smiled and caught Colin's hand.

Hannah hid a smile. She'd hoped Stacia would do this very thing, but they hadn't planned it.

Colin didn't want to be rude, so he skated away with Stacia. Wind blew through his sandy blond hair.

Across the pond Chelsea laughed as she watched Colin skate with Stacia. Maybe Colin would realize he was missing out on a lot of fun by keeping to himself all the time and worrying about aliens.

Just then Mike stopped beside Chelsea. "When are we going to have our talk with Colin?"

"After he's here for a while. I want him to see what he's missing by not having friends who don't live in fear." Chelsea watched Colin skate gracefully around the pond with Stacia. "He skates really well. I don't think he's been like he is now all his life."

"Did you notice that Colin never laughs?"

Chelsea nodded. "He doesn't even smile."

Mike squeezed Chelsea's hand. "I want to see him laugh."

"Me too. Let's talk to him right now." Chelsea skated over the ice with her hand wrapped around Mike's. They skated up to Stacia and Colin. Both had unzipped their jackets to cool off a bit.

Stacia smiled and said, "Hi. Colin, this is Chelsea and Mike McCrea. Chelsea helped plan this skating party."

"Hi, Colin," Chelsea and Mike said happily at the same time.

Colin frowned. How could they smile when they knew the danger? "I want to talk to you," he said sharply.

"Okay." Chelsea caught his free hand. "Do you mind, Stacia?"

"Go ahead. I'm going to find Brody and Duke. I hear we're supposed to perform today."

Chelsea nodded. "We can't wait to hear you."

Laughing, Stacia skated away. Mike took Colin's other hand.

Colin frowned at one, then the other. "What's going on?"

Laughing happily, Chelsea and Mike pulled Colin toward an empty bench far away from the bonfire and the cluster of skaters.

"We'll talk here," Chelsea said.

"We've got some really exciting stuff to tell you." Mike laughed as he carefully walked to the bench.

Colin frowned. Something was going on, but what? Mike wasn't frightened, and Chelsea seemed ready to burst with excitement. What had happened to them since he'd seen them last?

Chelsea plopped down onto the wooden bench

and waited for Colin and Mike to sit down too. Laughter exploded from several kids on the pond. All the bright colors on the ice were like looking in a kaleidoscope. Oh, but Colin was missing a lot by not being able to notice such beauty!

Laughing, Mike held his legs straight out. "Look, Colin. See my legs?"

"Yes." Colin frowned. "What about them?"

Mike patted his legs below his knees. "I still have 'em. Know what I did?"

Chelsea laughed under her breath. Mike was having a great time.

Mike looked squarely at Colin. "I walked and jumped and danced and ran all across the sunken ground where you said the spaceship landed. And nothing happened to me."

The color drained from Colin's face. "How could you do something so dangerous, Mike? You might wake up tomorrow without any legs."

"I won't," Mike said with great assurance.

Colin didn't know what to make of Mike. "Why aren't you scared like you were?"

"Because God is our Heavenly Father, and Jesus is our Savior, and angels watch over us and are stronger than aliens," Chelsea said happily.

Colin sucked in his breath. "I don't know who you've been talking to, but you're wrong! Nothing can stop the takeover, and nothing is more powerful than the aliens . . . Unless we all unite and fight to destroy them."

His face serious, Mike looked at Colin. "God is more powerful than aliens. God created the heavens and the earth and all that's in them. We belong to God. He takes care of us."

Chelsea nodded. "Satan came to destroy all of us, but Jesus defeated Satan. One of the Devil's weapons is fear. If we let fear rule us, anything can destroy us. The Bible says God gave us a spirit of love and power and a strong mind. He did not give us a spirit of fear, though our enemy Satan did. So that means we can reject fear and be free of it. Colin, you don't have to live in fear. Whether aliens are real or not has nothing to do with this. Fear is hurting you. I know you hate going to bed afraid and getting up each morning even more afraid."

Colin trembled. He did hate being afraid. But how could he live without fear? That's what kept him fighting against the terrible takeover. "You two just don't understand! I came to talk to Troy and John. If I can't talk to them right now, I'm going home."

Chelsea caught Colin's arm before he could move. "At least wait until Stacia sings. Colin, you never heard anything like it in your life! Please wait."

"Oh, all right!" The words surprised him. He'd planned to say he wouldn't stay no matter how much they begged. "But I want to talk to John and Troy."

Chelsea hesitated, then shrugged. "Okay. Come on." She knew the boys were having fun skating, even though they did worry about aliens.

A few minutes later Chelsea introduced Colin to John and Troy. She and Mike skated away, silently praying for Colin.

Troy skated backwards while he studied Colin. "I hear you've got proof aliens have landed."

Colin hesitated. Was Troy mocking him? "I might have."

"We want to see it," John said excitedly.

Colin told them where he lived. "Come over after school Monday, and I'll show you."

"We'll be there." The boys skated away, then joined two other boys who were having races.

Colin slowly skated toward the bench near the bonfire. What was happening to him? He could've taken the boys to his house right now to show them the thing he'd found. Mom and Dad were shopping, and the house was empty. Why hadn't he done it?

Just then Roxie skated up to Colin and caught his hand. "I've been watching you skate. You're good."

"Thanks."

"Want to be my partner for the pairs competition? We skate together for about three minutes while everyone watches. The couple who does the best together gets a prize."

Colin hesitated, then found himself saying, "Sure, I'll do it."

"We'll practice a few minutes and try to work out a routine."

Colin skated around with Roxie while they both suggested different moves they could make. Later they skated alone on the ice while everyone watched and cheered, and then they stood at the sidelines and watched others compete.

To Roxie's surprise Alyson Griggs and her partner, Bruce Keine, won. "They sure were good together."

Colin nodded.

Her eyes sparkling, Roxie smiled at Colin. "So we didn't win, but we had fun anyway, didn't we?"

"Yes." Colin turned quickly away. What was wrong with him? He didn't have time to have fun! "I gotta go," he said in a low, tight voice.

Roxie caught his arm. "No . . . Wait. Stacia's getting ready to sing. You've got to hear her! She's incredible!"

Colin wanted to jerk free and run home, but he stayed beside Roxie and listened to Stacia King sing while Brody and Duke played. The song was called "Mighty Conqueror," and it sent a thrill through Colin.

Was it possible that God was really stronger

than aliens and that He'd given them the power to be mighty conquerors?

The minute the song ended Roxie skated over to Stacia, but Colin pulled off his skates and tied his sneakers back on. He ran out of the park as fast as he could go.

He dare not forget his mission—to find a way to keep the aliens from taking over the world! That's all that mattered!

11

Colin

Colin slowly walked from the park to the woods near his house. He stood beside the indentation and looked across it. Why hadn't Mike been harmed by walking in it? Colin rubbed a hand over his hair. Had he been wrong about a spaceship landing here, or was Mike protected by angels?

Taking a deep breath, Colin stuck his foot out to step in the area, but he couldn't do it. He jumped back and almost fell in the snow. Something shiny caught his attention. His heart stopped, then thundered on. Slowly he bent down to brush the snow away from the object. It was a crystal about as big around as a large marble. He picked it up and held it in his palm. It was heavier than a marble and flashed different colors as the sun hit it. Had it come off a spaceship along with the other thing he'd found?

He closed his hand over it. Did it feel hot, or was it only his imagination?

Maybe there were more things. He kicked around in the snow, but he didn't see anything else except snow and dirt. He pushed his hand into the pocket of his jeans and let the crystal drop to the bottom of his pocket. Maybe the crystal was only an ordinary crystal, or maybe it wasn't. He'd have to be careful whom he showed it to in case it was from a spaceship.

He pulled it out of his pocket and held it in his hand.

"What did you find?"

Colin jumped at the sound of a voice. He looked up to see John and Troy walking toward him. Should he show them the crystal?

"We asked Chelsea where we could find you," Troy said as he looked nervously around.

"We didn't get to talk much a while ago." John stood with his hands in his jacket pockets. "Show us what you found."

"It might not be anything." Colin opened his hand and held it out. The crystal flashed bright colors. "It's a crystal."

The boys nodded as they studied it. Finally Troy picked it up. "It's heavy."

John backed away. "I wouldn't touch it in case it has powers we don't know about. I heard about a guy who found a strange-looking tool. He thought it was for a foreign car or something. When he touched it, it burned his hand so bad that he dropped it. When he went to get it again, it was gone. It just vanished . . . into thin air."

Colin shivered. It frightened him to hear such things, but it made him thankful that he wasn't the only one who knew aliens existed.

"He still has a scar today," John said.

Troy shoved the crystal back at Colin. "I sure don't want to be burned."

Colin pushed the crystal back into his pocket. "Do you guys know others who think aliens are taking over or are going to take over the world?"

"My dad says they will before the year is out," Troy said in a husky voice. He nervously fingered the zipper of his jacket. "He has only one friend who believes him. Everybody else laughs at him when he starts talking about aliens."

Colin thought about Chelsea and Mike. "Do you guys believe in God?"

"I guess," John said.

"Sure. Who doesn't?" Troy added.

"Could angels protect us from aliens?" Colin really wanted to know what John and Troy thought.

Troy shrugged. "I never thought about angels."

"Are they real?" John frowned thoughtfully.

"Chelsea says they're real." Colin felt funny talking about Chelsea and angels to the boys, but he had to know what they'd say.

Troy waved his hand to brush aside Colin's word. "There are some people who think that, but I don't."

"I wish it was true," John said.

Hope died inside Colin that he hadn't even realized was there. He talked a while longer to the other boys, then slowly walked alone to his house and around to the backyard. The sun had melted some of the snow, leaving bare patches here and there. He knew his parents were probably home by now, but he didn't want to go inside. They'd ask him all about the skating party. They were desperate for him to have fun with kids his age. During the past two and a half years since he'd learned the terrible truth about aliens, his mom and dad had been trying to get him to be like other kids. They couldn't understand why he stayed so much to himself or why he was so obsessed with outer space. They didn't realize how close to destruction they were, but he did.

Later in his room Colin set the crystal on his nightstand beside his alarm clock. He rubbed his finger over the crystal. If it was from the spaceship, would it call the alien right into his bedroom? He shivered. He didn't know if he could survive a visit from aliens.

Just then his door opened, and his dad walked in, smelling like he'd just eaten a salami sandwich. He was a tall, thin man with a big nose like Colin's. "You had a visitor while you were gone."

Colin stiffened. "Who?"

"Glenn McCrea. He says you know his kids—Chelsea and Mike."

Colin nodded and tried to hide his fear. Mr. McCrea's visit probably meant big trouble. "What did he want?" It was hard to talk around the knot in his throat.

"To meet you and to return a video you loaned his kids. I was worried he'd come to lambaste you for talking to his kids about this alien foolishness, but he didn't say a word about that."

Colin sank weakly onto his desk chair.

Colin's dad smiled. "He invited you to a valentine party at their house tomorrow evening at 5. I said you'd go."

"I can't!"

"You're going. Subject closed." Dad walked out of the room and left the door open behind him.

Colin groaned. How could he survive being at that party? Chelsea's friends were too friendly! He frowned. Was he expected to take valentine cards? He hadn't gone to a party since he was ten!

Suddenly he couldn't stand to be in his room a minute longer. He felt too closed in. He grabbed his jacket and hurried outdoors to the backyard. If he had a brother, would they talk about aliens or the valentine party?

He frowned. What a dumb thought.

Listlessly he walked around his yard. Why hadn't Chelsea's dad complained about him?

Just then Chelsea walked across her backyard and came up behind Colin in his yard. She wanted to tell him that she wanted to be friends, no matter how he felt about aliens. He looked depressed. "Hi," she said brightly.

He jumped in surprise. "Hi. Your dad came over while I was gone."

"I knew he wanted to talk to you."

"He invited me to the valentine party at your house tomorrow at 5."

"Great! I was going to see if you'd come too."

"Should I bring valentines for everybody or what?"

"Don't bring anything. We're going to play games and eat. It'll be fun. You met most of the kids who are coming at the skating party."

"I can't believe your dad didn't tell my dad about aliens and scaring you and Mike and all. Wasn't he mad?"

"He felt bad for us and for you."

"For me?" Colin's heart jerked strangely.

"He does want to talk to you. Come to our house, will you? He's in the study right now."

Colin wanted to refuse, but instead he found himself walking into the house with Chelsea. The house was warm and smelled like chocolate. His family never had chocolate at their house. Dad was allergic to it. Sometimes Colin and Mom would go out for dessert and go crazy over chocolate though.

"Want a cup of cocoa?" Chelsea asked.

Colin shook his head. He was too nervous to swallow.

Chelsea smiled as she led the way to the study. "Relax. Dad won't yell at you. Honest."

Colin took a deep breath and tried not to tremble as they walked into the study. Dressed in jeans and a blue sweatshirt, Glenn McCrea walked from behind his desk as if he were happy to see them. Colin tensed.

Glenn put an arm around Chelsea.

"Dad, this is Colin Mayhew."

Glenn held out his hand. Colin finally shook it, and Glenn said, "I'm happy to meet you."

"My dad said you came to see me." Colin sounded stiff, and he flushed.

"Sure did. Have a seat. You too, Chelsea."

Colin sat on the couch with Chelsea, while Glenn leaned back against his desk. Colin didn't know what to expect. Glenn McCrea was a lot different than his dad.

"I left your video at your house when I was there earlier. Did you get it?"

Colin nodded.

"I know you didn't realize the harm that video would cause my children, but watching violence does do damage to the one watching."

Chelsea sat in the corner of the couch so she could watch both Dad and Colin as Dad said almost the very same things he'd said to her and Mike.

Colin moved restlessly. What Mr. McCrea was saying sounded logical.

Glenn talked for several minutes, then said, "Do you have something to say, Colin?"

Colin's eyes widened. His dad never asked him that. Colin couldn't think of a thing. "I guess not," he said just above a whisper.

"Don't you want to know if aliens are real?" Chelsea asked.

Colin frowned. "I already know they're real."

"The Bible doesn't mention aliens." Glenn rubbed a finger over his mustache. "The Bible does talk about angels visiting Earth at different times, but it doesn't say whether there is life on other planets."

"How can you believe the Bible?" Colin flushed. "I'm sorry . . . I shouldn't have asked that."

"No, it's all right. I believe the Bible is God's Word. It was written by men of God who wrote what the Holy Spirit told them to write. God Himself created us and wants to be friends with us because He loves us. He knows we have strayed away from His commandments, but He is willing to forgive us." Glenn smiled at Colin. "God knows all about you, Colin. The Bible says God knows your name and the number of hairs on your head. You are valuable to Him. But there is an enemy, Satan, who wants to destroy you. He doesn't want you to know God or to have a relationship with Him. Satan will do everything he can to keep you away from God. Fear is one way."

Colin felt funny inside. It was hard to imagine that God knew his name and knew all about him.

Glenn picked up a Bible from his desk. "I'm giving you this, Colin. I marked some verses in here. Read this, especially the verses I marked. You'll see that what I've told you is true. You'll see that Jesus is willing to be your friend and your Savior."

Colin took the small black Bible and mumbled, "Thanks." A tingle ran over him as he looked at it. Was what Mr. McCrea said true?

"We want you to be happy," Chelsea said with a smile. "Mike and I know you don't have to be afraid all the time."

Colin didn't know what to say.

"Will you read the Bible?" Glenn pointed to the Bible in Colin's hand.

"Yes." Colin nodded. He'd heard about Jesus on TV and had wondered if what he'd heard was true.

"Dad, Colin's coming to the party tomorrow," Chelsea said.

"Good!"

Colin awkwardly stood up. "I might be busy tomorrow."

"But we want you to come! Don't we, Dad?"

"Of course. You'll enjoy it, Colin. But we won't force you. It's up to you."

Colin held the Bible close to him. "I'll come." His dad had said he had to attend, but Chelsea's dad said it was his decision.

Several minutes later, back in his own house, Colin closed his bedroom door, sat at his desk, and opened the Bible to the bookmark. Was it possible he'd find help just like Mr. McCrea had said?

12

Heather's Valentine Party

Chelsea stepped close to Hannah as they waited for Mrs. Robbins to answer the door. They were all thinking about seeing the two women who didn't like Native Americans. "We'll try to keep them away from you," Chelsea said softly.

Kathy and Roxie nodded. "We will."

"I almost didn't come." Hannah managed to smile. "But I decided I could handle it as long as you girls were with me."

The door opened, and Mrs. Robbins nervously beckoned them in. She wore red slacks and jacket with a satiny white blouse. "All the decorations are up, and the guests will be coming soon." Mrs. Robbins sounded impatient. "I was afraid you wouldn't come."

Chelsea smiled. "We said we would, and we

keep our word." They hung their jackets in the hall closet, and then Chelsea led the way to the basement where the party would be held. She knew the basement was Heather's special play area. In the winter she even rode her bike and roller-skated there.

Mrs. Robbins walked partway down the steps and stopped. "If you girls need anything, let me know."

"Thanks," Roxie said cheerfully. None of them were going to hold a grudge against Mrs. Robbins or her relatives.

"I'll send the children down as soon as they come. Heather's still in her room." Mrs. Robbins cleared her throat. "She doesn't think she'll have fun."

"Do you want me to talk to her?" Chelsea asked gently.

Mrs. Robbins nodded. "I'd appreciate it."

"I'll go up in a few minutes. I know where her room is."

"Thank you." Mrs. Robbins slowly walked back up and closed the door.

Chelsea turned to the Best Friends. "We'll hide the hearts first. Don't hide them too well—we want the kids to find them easily." The first game was to find the red paper hearts of different sizes hidden all over the basement. Then one at a time the kids would be blindfolded and stick their heart in the basket. Hannah had painted a big basket on a large piece of paper and was hanging it on the far wall. It was much like the old game "Pin the Tail on the Donkey," except they didn't use pins—they used a piece of rolled scotch tape on the back of each paper heart. Even if the kids missed the basket, the whole thing would make a good valentine party decoration.

A few minutes later Chelsea ran lightly up to the second floor to Heather's bedroom. It was a huge room with more stuffed animals than Chelsea had ever seen except when her own room had been full of the animals she'd made to sell at the Arts and Crafts Show. Heather was standing at her window with her back to the door. Her long dark hair was held back with two big, red barrettes. She wore a red skirt and vest and a white blouse with puffy sleeves.

"Hi, Heather."

The little girl looked over her shoulder with big, sad, brown eyes. "Hi, Chelsea. Are you getting my party ready?"

"Yes. I think you'll have a lot of fun."

Tears rolled down Heather's face. "No, I won't! Nobody likes me!"

"That isn't true. I know Hannah's sisters like you."

"My aunts are mad because they're coming. They said I shouldn't be friends with Indians."

Chelsea held back her anger as she slipped an arm around Heather. "I'm sorry they feel that way, but I know *you're* happy to have them as friends.

And they're excited about coming to the party. They should be here in about fifteen minutes."

Heather shivered. "I know I won't have fun. First I was happy about the party, but now I'm not."

Chelsea lifted Heather's face with her fingers under her chin. "Tell me what's really wrong."

"I'm not going to get any presents."

"This isn't a birthday party, you know."

"But I thought I was going to get presents."

"You'll have fun playing games with your guests. And you're going to get a heart-shaped cake with ice cream."

"I saw the cake, and it is pretty, and I do like ice cream. But I don't know how to play any games."

"We'll tell you how." Chelsea hugged Heather close. "You'll have fun."

Heather trembled. "I won't."

Chelsea suddenly realized Heather was afraid. It was strange the way fear could spoil things—even a valentine party.

Chelsea held Heather from her and looked intently down at her. "Heather, Jesus loves you, doesn't He?"

"Yes," she said in a tiny voice.

"He is always *always* with you, isn't He?"

"Yes."

"He will be with you at the party too. He'll

help you have fun, and He'll help you enjoy the guests."

"I'm sooo afraid!"

"I can pray with you right now so you won't be. Want me to?"

Heather nodded.

Chelsea pulled Heather close again and prayed, "Heavenly Father, thank You for Heather. In Jesus' name her fear is gone so she can enjoy her party. She'll know what to say and what to do because You're with her, Jesus. Help her show her guests she likes them and wants them to have fun. Amen."

Heather smiled and wiped away her tears. "I can have fun now. And I'll help the others to have fun—especially Lena and Sherry and Vivian. I don't care if they are Ottawa Indians!"

"I know you don't." Chelsea hugged Heather tight. "I'm going back downstairs to finish getting everything ready. See you soon."

"Thanks, Chelsea."

"You're very welcome." Chelsea smiled and hugged Heather again.

Later the basement seemed full of boys and girls between the ages of seven and nine. Some of the girls wore dresses, and others wore jeans. All the boys were in jeans. Nobody talked or even smiled. They all looked a little afraid.

Chelsea stood at the front of the room near the basket picture Hannah had hung up. "Hello, boys and girls. Welcome to this great valentine party. Heather wants all of you to have a good time. Roxie, Kathy, Hannah, and I—I'm Chelsea—are here to help you have fun. If you need the bathroom, it's right over there. We'll stay down here to play games, then go upstairs to eat later." Chelsea held up a paper heart. "We've hidden paper hearts all over the room. I want you to each find only one heart. As soon as you have your heart, go stand beside Roxie." Roxie held up her hand, and all the kids looked at her. "Even if you find several hearts, only pick up one. Leave the others for someone else."

Kathy stepped forward with a bell in her hand. "When I ring this bell, start looking for a heart. Get ready . . ." She held the handbell high and rang it. Suddenly the basement echoed with shouts and laughter as the kids searched for the hearts. It was as if the sound of the bell had broken the silence in everyone.

After three games Chelsea called for everyone to sit down. When they were all relatively quiet again she said, "As a special surprise today we've invited Stacia, Brody, and Duke to entertain you with their music." Chelsea had seen Kathy sneak them into the TV room while the kids were playing the last game. "Please welcome Stacia, Brody, and Duke!" Chelsea clapped, and the kids joined in.

Dressed in a white dress with hearts all over it,

Stacia ran to the front with Brody and Duke close behind, their guitars hanging on their backs. As everyone clapped, the boys started to play their guitars. The kids quieted down, and Stacia smiled, then sang a noisy, funny song.

Chelsea laughed along with the little kids. Her heart fluttered each time she looked at Brody. Then she realized that he glanced away each time their eyes met. She bit her lip. Did he think she didn't like him anymore? She'd tried to talk to him on the phone a couple of times since she'd seen him in school and had treated him so badly, but he wouldn't talk to her. Maybe before they left today she'd have a chance to speak to him. He just had to understand she hadn't been herself that day in school!

Anger at Colin for making her so afraid that she'd hurt Brody's feelings rose up in Chelsea. She knotted her fists and thought of all the things she could say to Colin if he were here right now. Then she remembered that Jesus wanted her to be kind to Colin, no matter what he'd done to her. She had to choose between doing what Jesus wanted or following her feelings. She chose to obey Jesus. She silently asked Jesus to forgive her for her anger at Colin, and then she let the anger ooze out of her until once again she could enjoy the music and the party. It was always better to obey Jesus!

Brody glanced at Chelsea, and she smiled. He

looked quickly away. She smiled wider. She'd make sure he knew she did like his valentine and that she did like him.

Later she sent the kids upstairs to eat under the supervision of Heather's mom and aunts. Chelsea searched for Brody, but before she could speak to him he was gone. Her heart sank, but she quickly determined that she wasn't going to be upset! She'd find a way to talk to Brody and set things right.

"Time to clean up," Kathy said, making a face as she looked around at the mess. She picked up scattered red paper hearts and dropped them in a black, plastic garbage bag.

Hannah glanced uneasily up the steps. "I wonder if Heather's aunts are making trouble for my sisters. I hope not."

Roxie looked up from putting away the few toys the kids had managed to get out even though they were told not to. "Did you tell your sisters about the aunts?"

Hannah shook her head. "I thought it would be better not to. They don't even know they weren't supposed to be invited."

Chelsea carefully took the picture of the basket off the wall. Some of the hearts fell on the floor, and she picked them up. "Did you notice Brody wouldn't even look at me?"

The girls shook their heads. "We were too busy watching Stacia sing," Kathy said. "How I wish I could sing like she does! My dad says he's going to try to get her on his show as a guest singer." Kathy's dad was head musician on a Christian TV program. "He said the right person might hear her and give her a record deal. That would be great, wouldn't it?"

The others agreed, and they talked about that as they finished cleaning.

Suddenly the basement door burst open, and Hannah's sister Lena ran downstairs, her dark eyes flashing. "They said it, Hannah!" she cried, grabbing Hannah's arm.

"Said what?" Hannah's stomach knotted as the Best Friends gathered around.

Lena took a deep breath. "Heather's aunts said the only good Indian was a dead Indian. Then they laughed."

Chelsea had heard that saying all her life, ever since she'd lived around Indians in Oklahoma. She knew it was a cruel thing to say to Lena and the twins. "Let's go upstairs and do something!"

"We don't want to cause trouble," Hannah said as she patted Lena on the back to comfort her.

Roxie started up the steps. "We can at least be with the twins."

"And stop the aunts from saying anything else," Kathy said.

Chelsea followed the Best Friends and Lena upstairs to the dining room, where the kids all sat around the big table eating cake and ice cream. The twins were sitting side by side, but they weren't eating. The empty chair beside them was where Lena had been sitting. Vanilla ice cream was melting into the half-eaten chocolate cake. Mrs. Robbins and two women were standing by the door that led into the kitchen. They stopped talking as the girls walked around the table.

Lena sat back down, and the Best Friends stood behind her and the twins. They looked at the aunts.

Hannah bent down to the twins. "You can eat," she said softly.

They slowly picked up their spoons and took bites of ice cream.

Chelsea lifted her chin and squared her shoulders. "We wanted to make sure everyone was having a good time."

The aunts flushed and hurried into the kitchen. Mrs. Robbins cleared her throat. "I'm sorry . . ." She ducked into the kitchen without saying why she was sorry, but the Best Friends knew.

A few minutes later Mrs. Robbins and the aunts walked back in, carrying plates of ice cream and cake for the Best Friends. They took them, smiled, and said, "Thank you."

Heather scooted to the side of her chair. "Roxie, you can share my chair."

Smiling, Roxie sat with Heather, while Chelsea,

Kathy, and Hannah shared chairs with the twins and Lena.

Chelsea nudged Lena. "This is good cake and ice cream, isn't it?"

Lena smiled and nodded.

Kathy swallowed her bite and said, "Stacia King sure can sing, can't she?" Soon she had the kids talking about Stacia and music.

Chelsea sighed in relief. The party was a success despite the aunts being mean to the twins and Lena.

A few minutes later Heather jumped up. "Who wants to build a snowman in my front yard?"

The kids shouted, "We do!"

Chelsea motioned to the Best Friends that it was time to go. They told Mrs. Robbins good-bye and slowly walked down the street toward home. Snow sparkled in the sunlight. Water dripped from rows of icicles hanging off the roofs of the houses they passed.

"Three more hours and it'll be time for the party at my house." Chelsea's nerves tightened. Would she really have the courage to tell Brody how she felt about him?

13

Chelsea's Party

With a long sigh Chelsea read the valentine again that she'd bought for Brody while her mind had been full of fear of aliens. She leaned back on her chair and looked at the card from him to her propped open on her desk. The card for Brody wasn't what she'd buy now that she was thinking clearly. Should she give it to him anyway? It was a card she could give to Rob or Hannah or practically anybody else. It wasn't a special card like she'd wanted for Brody. She slapped it down on her desk. Why hadn't she looked at it again before it was too late to buy another one?

Her phone rang, and she almost fell off her chair. She scooped it up and breathlessly said, "Hello."

"Chelsea, it's Colin."

"Hi! What's up?"

"I can't come to your party."

"What's wrong?"

"I don't fit in with all of you. You know I don't."

Chelsea was silent a while. He didn't fit in, but she still wanted him to be there. "Please come, Colin. If you start feeling really uncomfortable you can go home."

"I guess."

"It's not as if you live across town. It's only across our backyard. Come on, Colin. You can do it."

He was quiet a long time. "I don't know what to wear. My mom says I should wear my suit and tie."

Chelsea bit back a laugh. "We'll all be wearing jeans. Tell your mom that, and she'll let you wear jeans."

"I hope so. See you later." Colin hung up and walked slowly to the bathroom across from his bedroom. He looked in the mirror above the sink and made a face. What a big nose! Why'd he inherit his dad's nose? Too bad he couldn't have plastic surgery before five o'clock.

He stepped out of the bathroom just as his mom started down the hall. She was small with blonde hair and a nice nose. Too bad he didn't have her nose. "Mom, I called Chelsea. She said they're all wearing jeans. So I'm wearing jeans."

"Do you have clean ones?"

"I guess so." Sometimes he wore the same pair for a week without thinking if they were dirty or not. He had to wear dress pants to private school, but after school each day he'd change into jeans.

"Let's go look." Mom put her hand on his arm. She was only two inches taller than he was. "I want to pick out your shirt too."

Colin bit his lip and kept quiet. He should've asked Chelsea about a shirt. She knew more about these things than Mom did.

In his room Colin opened his closet. It looked almost empty. He'd grown just before they'd moved, so they gave away his old shirts. He tugged at the sleeve of a blue shirt. "How about this one?"

Mom frowned as she glanced over his few shirts. "I don't suppose a white one would work."

"I don't think so. I like the blue one." Actually he didn't care if he liked his clothes or not. They were necessary to his existence, so he had them.

"Wear the blue one." Mom turned from the closet and glanced around the room. She spotted the crystal and picked it up. "How pretty!"

Colin froze. He didn't want to talk about it.

"My grandma had an elegant chandelier over her dining room table when I was a little girl. It had dozens of crystals like this hanging from it." She smiled. "I'd sit and watch it for hours and imagine all kinds of things—like they were really diamonds, but I was the only one who knew it. I'd think of all the things I could buy with the money I'd make by selling the diamonds. Mostly I wanted a horse."

Colin looked at Mom in surprise. She'd never told him that before. She hardly ever talked about her childhood.

She held the crystal up to the sunlight streaming through the window. "See the tiny hole down through it? I believe this is from a chandelier or a lamp."

His nerves tight, Colin peered closely at it. He hadn't noticed the hole before. Was it possible the crystal was what Mom had said instead of something from a spaceship?

She set the crystal back in place, then noticed the Bible. She picked it up and opened it to the bookmark. "I didn't know you had a Bible."

Colin sank to his chair. "Mr. McCrea gave it to me to read."

"How nice of him! I see he marked verses of importance." Mom silently read a few, then looked at Colin. "When I was your age I read the Bible every single day. I prayed and went to church too."

Colin hadn't known that either. "Why did you quit?"

"I guess I let it all slip away when I went to college. When I married your dad, he didn't have any interest in church or the Bible, so I let it slide even further away from me. I'm sorry I did now. I can remember having such peace when I prayed." She held the Bible close to her. "I haven't felt peace like that in a long, long time."

"Do you believe the Bible is true?"

"Of course I do!"

"Does Dad?"

Mom shrugged. "I don't know if he does or not. I think I'll ask him. In fact, I'm going to dig my Bible out and start reading it again."

"Maybe we could read it together," Colin said hopefully.

"I'd like that." Mom laid the Bible on the desk. "I accepted Jesus as my Savior when I was eleven years old. I wanted the whole world to do the same." She chuckled. "I went around telling everyone about Jesus. My mom and dad got embarrassed over my zeal, so finally I quit telling others. I wish I'd kept right on doing it." She held Colin's hand in hers. "I want you to know Jesus as your Savior, Colin! That's what's missing in your life. Why didn't I recognize that sooner?"

Hope rose in Colin as he listened to Mom talk about Jesus.

Finally she glanced at the clock and gasped, "It's time for you to dress and get over to the McCreas'. Have fun at the party."

Colin's mouth turned dust-dry. How could he have fun?

◼

Chelsea stood at the door and greeted the Best

Friends excitedly. They'd come a few minutes early so they could welcome the guests as they came. She was expecting fifteen kids at the party. She'd had a longer list, but Mom had trimmed it down to keep the house from exploding with noise.

Chelsea pulled Kathy aside and whispered, "Is Brody coming?"

Kathy nodded. "He and Duke will be here in a few minutes. They're going to walk here with Stacia and decide for sure what songs they'll do."

"Did he say anything about . . . about me?"

"No. Maybe he did to Duke, but not to me." Kathy patted Chelsea's back. "Don't worry about Brody. Have fun no matter what."

Chelsea finally nodded. "I will! But it'll be hard."

She thought of that later when Brody walked in with Duke and Stacia. Chelsea tried to get Brody to talk to her, but he slipped away and hurried down to the basement with Duke and Rob.

Just then Colin walked in, looking nervous and ready to run away. Chelsea took his jacket and added it to the pile inside the closet. "You can go on down if you want."

The color drained from Colin's face. "Could I stay here with you?"

"Sure. I won't be much longer." The doorbell rang, and she opened the door to let in Kesha Bronski.

Her blonde curls danced on her shoulders as she handed her jacket to Chelsea. "I'm sorry I'm late."

"No problem." Chelsea turned to Colin. "Kesha, this is a new friend—Colin. He lives behind us."

"I'm glad to meet you, Colin. We're going to have a great time tonight, aren't we?" Her teeth flashed as she smiled a wide smile, and her brown eyes sparkled.

Colin wanted to grab his jacket and run. Here was another overly-friendly friend of Chelsea's! Could he possibly survive this party?

Chelsea led Colin and Kesha to the basement that they'd decorated special for the valentine party. The room buzzed with talk and exploded with laughter. Four kids were already playing Ping-Pong, and four were playing pool, while two sat in front of the big-screen TV playing a video game. Kesha ran off to join Stacia at a board game.

Colin gulped. "I better go home."

"Please don't!" Chelsea gripped his arm and pulled him toward Hannah, who was starting a game of Clue. They both joined in.

To Colin's surprise he enjoyed the game. He liked pitting his deductive reasoning skills against Hannah's. She was good!

Much later Chelsea got Brody's card from the drawer in the basement kitchenette where she'd hidden it earlier, then walked among the guests until she found Brody. He was watching a game of pool. "Could we talk?" she asked softly.

He stiffened.

"Please." The card felt as heavy as an encyclopedia. "Please?"

He finally nodded.

She led him to an empty corner. "I have to explain about the other day in school."

His dark eyes were cold as he shook his head. "Don't bother."

"Please listen, Brody. I wasn't myself that day. I was scared about something dreadful happening, and that's all I could think about. I was glad to get your card. I wanted it a lot! I'm really really sorry I couldn't tell you. I read your card, and I liked it! I was sooo glad you put it in my locker!"

"You really liked it?"

"Yes!" She smiled. "I got one for you too. It's not as nice as yours to me. Here!" She thrust it into his hands.

He took it and opened it, then laughed as he read it. "Thanks. I like it."

"You do?" She felt weak with relief.

"Yeah, I do." He smiled.

His smile made her feel great! "Want to play a game?"

"Sure." He looked at the card again, stuffed it

back in the envelope, and pushed it into his back pocket. "Will you sit with me when we eat?"

"Sure." Chelsea felt as if she were floating up to the ceiling along with the balloons as she walked across the floor beside Brody. She couldn't wait to tell the Best Friends. They'd be as happy for her as she was. Best friends are like that.

14

The Smile

Colin took the bowl of vanilla ice cream with two heart-shaped cookies from Hannah. He'd planned to go home long before this, but he just couldn't break away. He was actually enjoying being with everyone, especially Hannah. He hadn't thought about aliens for the past three hours. A bite of cookie lodged in his throat. Aliens! How could he so easily forget the destruction coming to all of them? Could he tolerate seeing all of these kids destroyed and not telling them just because he wanted to have a little fun?

Abruptly he jumped up off the floor and headed for the stairs. He had to get home before he forgot how urgent his mission was. He rushed up the steps, then suddenly realized he was still carrying the bowl. Helplessly he looked at it. He would set it in the kitchen upstairs.

Just as he reached the top step, Hannah called

to him. He looked over his shoulder to find her running up the stairs after him. His heart sank. What could he say to her?

She reached his side and stepped into the hallway with him. "What's wrong, Colin?"

"I have to get out of here." He knew he sounded frantic, but he couldn't help it. He *felt* frantic.

"I can see you're frightened. Did somebody say something mean to you?"

He looked into her black eyes and suddenly couldn't think of a thing to say.

"Can we talk?" she asked softly. She'd had a great time with him, and she didn't want him to leave feeling upset.

He shrugged. "I guess."

She took his bowl and carried it to the kitchen. No one was there, so they sat at the table. "Can you tell me what frightened you so suddenly?"

"You wouldn't understand."

"Is it about aliens?"

He gasped. "What about them?"

"Chelsea told me about your fear."

"No!"

"She's concerned about you. I was really upset when I saw how terrified she was about aliens taking over the world. After she realized that God was with her no matter what, she stopped being afraid."

Hannah leaned forward slightly. "Colin, you don't have to be afraid either."

"I don't know what to say."

"Jesus loves you, Colin. He wants to protect you and care about you, but He can't if you won't let Him."

"I know." Colin rubbed his hand nervously over his cheek. "But I found a place where aliens landed! I know it's the truth!"

"Show me the place."

"It's too dark out."

"Show me after school tomorrow. I'll help you solve the mystery."

"I have proof in my room too."

"Show me the proof. I'll help you solve that mystery too."

Colin nervously rubbed his hands up and down his legs. "What if you discover there really are aliens?"

Hannah shrugged. "What if I discover that the place where they landed was made by something from *this* planet?"

"I'll still have the proof in the box in my room."

"What if I prove that's something made here too?"

Colin's heart raced so hard, he could barely catch his breath. Did he want her to prove it? "I'll meet you in my backyard right after school tomorrow."

"I'll be there." Hannah smiled. "Now, can we go back downstairs? Stacia is going to sing now."

Colin hesitated, then agreed. He walked down with Hannah and sat on the floor beside her as Stacia, Brody, and Duke performed. He'd never heard music that touched his heart like theirs.

Across the room Chelsea sat with her arms around her legs and her chin on her knees. Brody could play guitar sooo well! And he sang better than anyone she'd heard on her cassettes. When the songs ended, Chelsea clapped so long that her hands stung. She didn't want the music to end. She didn't want the party to end either, but it was time. They all had school tomorrow. And she and the Best Friends still had to clean up.

While everyone was saying good-bye, Chelsea tried to find a way to be alone with Brody for only a few minutes, but he was surrounded with admirers. She finally had to give up. She led them all upstairs for their jackets and said good-bye as they left. She handed Brody his jacket, and their hands brushed. "I'm glad you came, Brody."

"Me too."

"I'll talk to you soon." She wanted to say a whole lot more, but she knew she'd have a chance another day.

"See ya." He smiled, and it felt like a promise.

She wanted to say she liked him a lot, but she couldn't with others listening and waiting for their jackets. He walked out with a quick good-bye.

Suddenly she realized Colin was gone. She'd have to make sure to see him tomorrow to tell him she was glad he came.

At long last Chelsea walked slowly back downstairs where the Best Friends were already cleaning. The special rec room seemed too quiet after several hours of talking, laughing, singing, and shouting.

Chelsea suddenly felt too tired to stack the games away in the closet, but she did it anyway. She knew the girls were as tired as she was. It had been a long day—church that morning, Heather's party in the afternoon, then her party.

Finally everything was back in order. Chelsea smiled at her friends as they sank to the floor in a circle. They wanted to rest a bit and talk for a while. Chelsea patted their knees. "Thanks for helping."

"It was a fun party," Hannah said. Kathy and Roxie agreed.

Chelsea hooked her hair behind her ears. "I'm glad Colin came."

"Me too!" Hannah's eyes sparkled as she told them she was going to meet Colin after school and why. "So, I thought you girls should be there too. We can work together to help Colin."

"Good idea," Chelsea said.

Roxie clasped her hands together and sighed

happily. "I sat with Rob to eat tonight. I think he does like me! We talked and talked."

Chelsea giggled. "I remember when we first moved in, Rob really liked you, but I thought you were mean. I'm sure glad we became friends."

Roxie nodded. "Especially if Rob and I go together. Well, you know what I mean. We can't really go out or anything, but we can be together at parties."

"We know," Hannah said. None of them could actually go on a date until they were sixteen. They all thought that was too long to wait, but their parents were sure it wasn't. It was like their parents all had a meeting and came to the same conclusion, then stuck to it.

"I talked to Rob's friend Nick Rand a lot tonight." Kathy grinned sheepishly. "I didn't use to like him at all, but he's really nice. Rob says he's okay, so I guess he is."

"He is." Chelsea flushed. "I liked him for a while when we first moved here. Mike plays with Nick's little brother."

"We played Ping-Pong together." Kathy giggled. "I beat him, but he didn't get mad or anything. He says he's more into computers."

They talked a while longer, then had to say good night. It was always hard to leave each other, but knowing they'd see each other in school made it easier. "We'll meet right here tomorrow after school." Chelsea led them upstairs. "Be sure to keep praying for Colin. We don't want him to be afraid another day."

"That's for sure." Hannah slipped on her jacket. She liked him as much as she'd ever liked Eli Shoulders. That was a big surprise to her. She'd thought she'd never like anyone after Eli. "See you tomorrow."

Chelsea opened the door and gasped at the rush of icy air. She was ready for winter to be over.

■

The next day after school the Best Friends walked to Colin's yard where he was waiting.

"We all came," Chelsea said with a laugh. "We all want to work together to solve this mystery."

Colin shrugged. "I already know what I know, but I'll show you the place where the spaceship landed—and this . . ." He held up the box he'd kept hidden under his bed. He hadn't brought the crystal because he had a feeling it was just what his mom had said. But the thing in the box was different. He was convinced it wasn't of this world.

A few minutes later Colin and the Best Friends stood in the very spot where Colin was sure a spaceship had landed. "This is it," he said with a catch in his voice. All of a sudden, thinking a spaceship had landed there seemed ludicrous to him. Could it be what Chelsea's dad had said—was Satan using this to deceive him so he'd live in fear?

The girls looked at the spot in the woods without speaking. Finally Roxie turned toward the house that was being built. She saw a pickup and a man loading tools in the back. She turned back to the indentation. "My dad is a building contractor, so I've been to building sites lots of time. This looks like a place where a front end loader dug up some dirt. Let's go ask that man working at the house. My dad knows him. His name is Doug Fairfield."

Trembling, Colin followed the girls to the house. Was it going to be this easy? Had he lived in fear because he had desperately wanted to believe in aliens?

Roxie shouted to the man as he opened his pickup door. He was getting ready to leave for the day, and she had to settle this now.

Doug Fairfield turned to the kids and pushed his cap to the back of his head. He wore a brown canvas coat, overalls, and heavy boots. "What's up, kids?"

"I'm Roxie Shoulders. You know my dad Burt."

"Sure do."

"We saw an indentation in the woods over there, and I thought it was made by a front end loader. Am I right?"

Doug chuckled. "Is there a bet going on here?"

"Sort of," Chelsea said.

Doug nodded. "I needed some fill dirt, and I

scooped a little from the woods where it wouldn't show."

Colin almost dropped his box. A spaceship had not landed there!

"Colin has something to show you." Hannah nudged Colin. "He found it in the woods near the spot where you dug."

"Let me have a look."

Colin reluctantly opened the box and lifted out the piece.

Doug chuckled and took it from Colin. "My boy has been looking for this. We were working together on it, and he was sure he left it around here somewhere, but it just up and disappeared."

Colin knew the man wasn't making the story up. Relief washed over him, leaving him weak in the knees.

"What is it anyway?" Chelsea asked.

"We're building a small racing car, and that's part of the fender. It's made of aluminum, plexiglass, and plastic. Tommy needs the car to be as light as possible, so we tried using those materials. He's sure gonna be glad to get this back."

"I didn't know it belonged to anyone," Colin said weakly.

"No problem." Doug set the object on the front seat of his pickup. "Any more questions?"

"No."

"Then I'll be going home. Tell your dad I said hello."

Roxie nodded. "I will."

Doug drove away, and no one said anything for a long time.

Colin kicked at a frozen clump of dirt. "I really feel dumb."

"Don't!" Hannah cried. She smiled at him. "Now that you know the truth, don't you feel better?"

Colin thought about the home video he'd watched and about John and Troy whom he'd met ice-skating yesterday. He suddenly realized they hadn't come to see him like they'd said they'd do. Maybe they didn't believe in aliens as much as they'd said. "What about others who say aliens are real?"

Chelsea cocked her head and studied Colin. "Remember what my dad said—aliens or no aliens, you can't let fear rule your life. God wants you to be free to love Him and free to enjoy life."

"That's right," the others said.

"We've been praying for you." Hannah pushed her long hair over her shoulder and smiled. "We want you to know Jesus as your personal Savior."

"Me too." Colin swallowed hard. "I read the Bible verses and talked to my mom. She said she knows I need Jesus in my life."

"We can pray with you right now," Chelsea

said. She knew Mike would've loved to be here to see this, but he'd gone to a friend's house after school.

Colin looked around. "Here? Now?"

"Sure." Hannah blinked back a tear. "Jesus doesn't care where you are when you invite him to be your friend and Savior."

Colin shrugged. "Okay . . . Right here . . . Right now."

They bowed their heads, and Hannah helped Colin pray, "Jesus, I want You to be my Savior and to forgive me of anything I've done that made You sad. Help me to do what You want me to do from this day forward. I give myself to You. I accept you as my friend and Savior. Amen."

As Colin prayed the words after Hannah prayed them, he felt a heavy weight lift off his heart. He felt the darkness that had surrounded him for so long *vanish*. The fear he'd lived with for two and a half years was gone! Incredible! He looked at the girls in awe. His eyes sparkled. "I'm no longer afraid!"

"You're a new creature in Christ Jesus," Kathy said softly.

Chelsea saw the light in Colin's eyes and on his face. Suddenly he smiled, then laughed right out loud. Tears welled up in Chelsea's eyes. Colin had smiled! Colin had actually laughed!

"This is great!" Colin tipped back his head and

laughed again. "This is really great! Wait'll I tell my mom!"

"Will she be home yet?" Hannah asked.

Colin looked at his watch and nodded.

"Then go tell her! We'll see you later or after school tomorrow."

Colin started away, then turned back. "Thanks."

Smiling, Chelsea shrugged. "What are friends for?"

"Friends?" Colin could barely get the word out. He hadn't had a friend since he was nine.

"Friends," the girls all said at the same time.

"Special friends," Hannah said softly.

"Thanks." Colin turned away so they wouldn't see the tears in his eyes. He had friends—real friends! And Hannah was his special friend! It was too good to be true, yet he knew it really was true.

The Best Friends slowly walked to Chelsea's yard. They looked at each other and laughed. They were happy beyond words about Colin. They didn't need to say anything. Each knew what the other was thinking. Best friends are like that.

You are invited to become a
Best Friends Member!

In becoming a member you'll receive a club membership card with your name on the front and a list of the Best Friends and their favorite Bible verses on the back along with a space for your favorite Scripture. You'll also receive a colorful, 2-inch, specially-made I'M A BEST FRIEND button and a write-up about the author, Hilda Stahl, with her autograph. As a bonus you'll get an occasional newsletter about the upcoming BEST FRIENDS books.

All you need to do is mail your NAME, ADDRESS (printed neatly, please), AGE and $3.00 (U. S. currency only) for postage and handling to:

BEST FRIENDS
P.O. Box 96
Freeport, MI 49325

WELCOME TO THE CLUB!

(Authorized by the author, Hilda Stahl)